# SPIRITUAL WARFARE

## BY

## CANDACE PAUL

SPIRITUAL WARFARE

Copyright © 2016 by Candace Paul



ISBN: 978-1-7333675-3-0


Aknowingspirit, LLC
P.O. Box 3324
Washington, DC 20010

www.aknowingspirit.com
Ordering Information:
Quantity sales. Special discounts are available on quantity purchases by churches, associations, and others. For details, contact the publisher at the address above.
Orders by U.S. trade bookstores and wholesalers. Please contact via www.aknowingspirit.com.

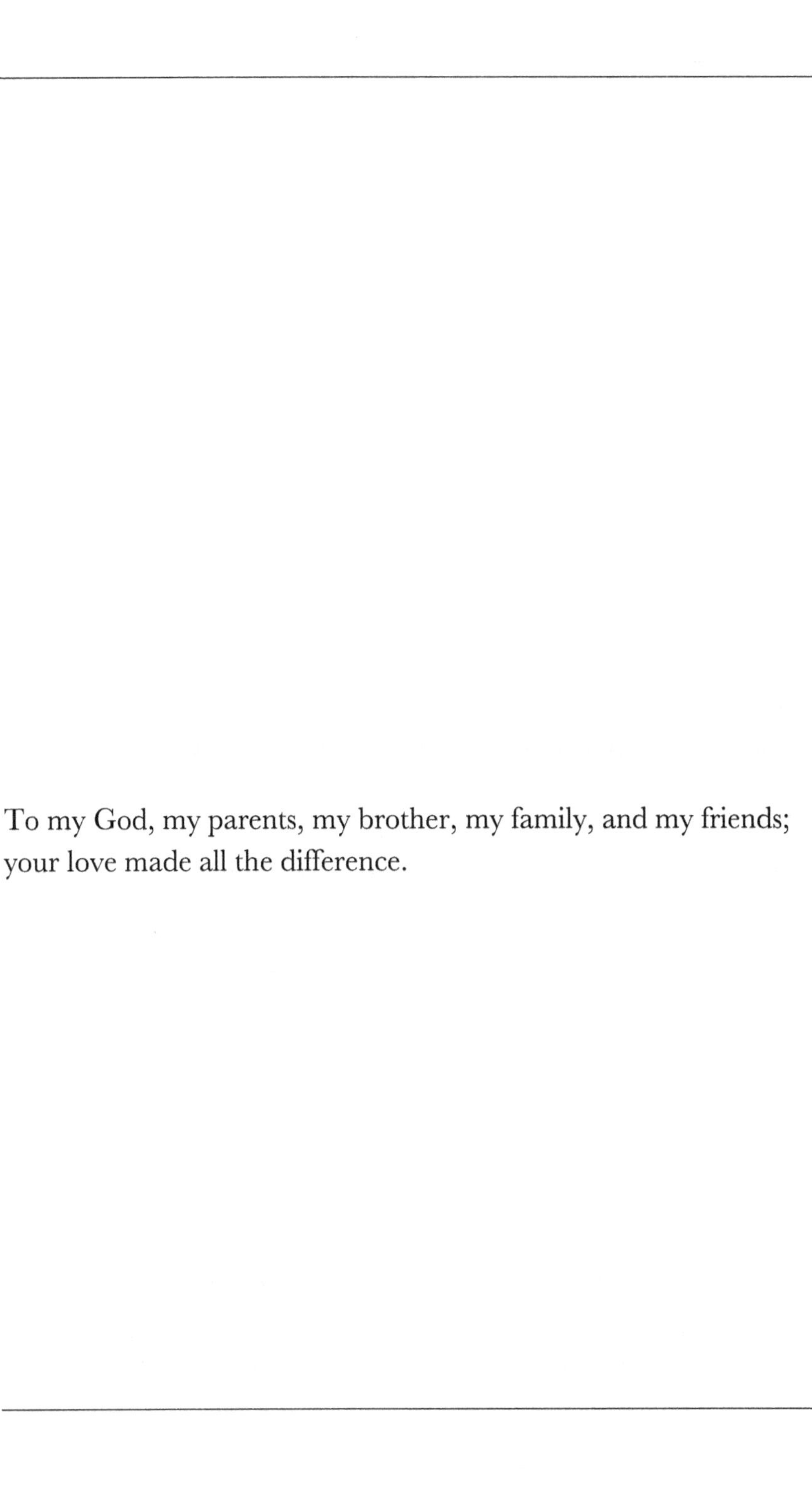

To my God, my parents, my brother, my family, and my friends; your love made all the difference.

# **<u>Foreward</u>**

There have been moments throughout my life when I just knew God was real. It was more than just a feeling—an event only I understood, confirmed it. These moments are difficult to explain, and in many ways, difficult for others to understand. While they made perfect sense to me, I may never be able to fully convey how, in those moments, I knew God was real. Fortunately, my responsibility is not to convince others that my personal experiences with God are real. Instead, I am called simply to encourage others to develop a personal relationship with God on their own. God will do the rest.

For me, every time God did something extraordinary in my life, things began to connect. I understood why events happened or didn't happen, why certain friendships ended, and why unlikely friendships began. Those moments that seemed like mere coincidences, failures, and missed opportunities all started to fit together. Each moment of my life was like a cobblestone. They varied in shape and size—some stood out and had greater significance than others. Some stones had glaring imperfections, while others appeared to be more polished. Some stones represented moments of despair, while others represented moments of hope. When I was too close, each stone—like each moment in my life—looked arbitrary. It seemed as if any stone could have been placed anywhere, and it would have all been the same. God showed me this wasn't true.

It was only until I took a step back to look at the ground as a whole and saw far into the distance that my path became clear. Not only was the collective cobblestone a beautiful collage of my life and unique experiences, each stone was a part of a purposeful design by the Creator used for my preordained path to Him.

I am not alone. I believe we all have our own cobblestone-path designed by God, but we must choose to walk it. It requires that we put the past under our feet and use it only to prop us up and keep us grounded. It requires that we forsake all other paths. We may trip, we may fall, but we must keep moving forward toward God on the path.

Still, walking on God's path is hard to do when the world leads us to believe that there is no path. The world makes us think that our lives are nothing more than a collection of random events, that are comprised of luck and chance. The world tries to convince us that the people we meet, the relationships we build, the talents we have, the places we go, and the things we see, were all just as likely to happen as they were not.

The intention of this book is for you, the reader, to contemplate the possibility that nothing is left to chance. That each day, much of what we see and hear is priming us to accept one of three beliefs: 1) God doesn't exist, 2) If He does exist, He doesn't have to be a priority, or 3) You can believe in anything you want and somehow this will be pleasing to God.

It may not seem like this is the goal—since much of what we see and hear fails to mention God. But that's the point. Keeping God out of the conversation is the most effective way to prevent people from seeking Him. When we become inundated with other things—entertainment, careers, or status—when will we find time to contemplate His existence? If we believe in Him, when will we find time to make Him a priority? When will we find time to truly consider what He wants from us? If we become transfixed on everything else, we will never stop to ask the questions that matter most. That might be enough for the opposition.

If you take the time to think about creation—how and why everything started—it will undoubtedly lead to other questions—many of which will go unanswered in your lifetime. For me, as I began to seek answers to these questions, I decided not to limit myself to what the world has adopted as "truth." Instead, I decided to also consider what the world has strongly rejected as truth: The Bible.

I wanted to know what was so wrong with the text. If I took the time to read and understand the context of what was written, how would I be harmed? It was just information, right? As I began this journey, I started developing a deep sense of appreciation for other people, myself, and the earth. I also started to understand the meaning of patience, sacrifice, standards, contentment, and obedience.  Interestingly enough, the questions I thought would never be answered were revealed to me rather quickly. But I wanted to know something else: Who wanted to keep me from contemplating God in the first place? Why was it so important for me to be distracted for so long? Why do the people that control so much of what I see, hear, and read want to keep God out of the conversation? What do they believe? Do they want me to believe in the same thing?

As I started to see how I was being misled, and once it became clear to me, He was real, I developed a strong desire to do more for God. But before I could get started, I had to do a few things:

The first thing I needed to do was to continue to increase my knowledge of God. Growing up, and even for most of my adult life, I simply listened to what others told me regarding the Bible. So, when people vehemently doubted the truth of the Bible, I didn't have enough information to know one way or the other. It wasn't until I started reading the Bible on my own that I began to understand the context in which many of the stories were written and the meaning behind them.

The second thing I had to do was develop a strong support system—find other believers. I was blessed enough to have a few very good friends that had been walking the path God designed for a while, so I was able to ask them questions. Once they determined I had an interest in knowing God, they invited me to church, Bible Studies, or events just to fellowship with other believers. It showed me that I was not alone. There were others who felt the same way and we had a shared understanding. It was incredibly important that I knew this.

Next, I had to develop a prayer life. If I knew God was real, I needed to talk to Him. I needed to find time away from the television, the phone, and the internet just to be in quiet prayer with Him.

Last, but certainly not least, I actually had to start the process of implementing what I learned and what I believed into my life. I had to begin the hard work of turning away from sin—stumbling would happen without question, but I had to get right back up and press forward until I was strong enough not to look back anymore.

If you are feeling misled by the world, I encourage you to read and research for yourself. No matter where you are in your walk with God—even if you are struggling with your faith or even if you don't believe but are still open to considering a different perspective, God will still speak to you. If you feel in your heart that now is the time to seek God, to build a relationship with Him, to ask those difficult questions, go ahead and do it. As long as you're still breathing, it's never too late.

*"They will throw them into the blazing furnace, where there will be weeping and gnashing of teeth." Matthew 13:42*

# Chapter One

## Thrown

A man I did not recognize hovered over me. I smelled cigar and various ales on his breath. He was very close to my face—if I lifted my head, or he tilted his downward, our lips would have touched. Yet he sounded distant as if he were speaking from across the room. "Sir, are you alright? Can you hear me?" He yelled while his strong hands gripped my lapels. He forcefully shook my body. I could tell he desperately wanted my attention, but why? I was there—listening to every word and screaming at the top of my lungs, "I'm fine—I hear you!" Why couldn't he hear me?

A woman I knew gasped. "Is that Jade?" she asked a man standing next to her.

He nodded.

A crowd started to gather. Each person looked down at me. Some people looked horrified, while most seemed indifferent, or just curious. The frantic man's movements began to slow like someone placed stained glass over my eyes. My vision was blanketed with spots that grew larger, until I could only see white. The man was no longer visible; I could hear his voice echoing and the onlookers chattering. Soon that also grew faint, and I could no longer hear him or anything. For the first time, I tasted blood in my mouth. Was that my blood? I felt my chest expanding and my lungs gradually filling with liquid. It was getting harder to breathe! Each eyelid fought to remain open. I took a deep breath. I tried to take in as much air as my lungs would allow. Then I exhaled. I immediately knew that was the last time. My heart stopped beating, and everything went black.

***

I was alone—surrounded by total darkness. Was I dreaming? I was unable to see even an inch in front of my face or even see the ground. I quickly rose to my feet, stretching my arms out in an effort to aid my sight. I wanted to find a wall or a tree or anything I could rest my hand upon.

"Is anyone there? HELLO?!?" I screamed. No one answered. "WHERE AM I?!" There was only the sound of my frightened voice echoing in the darkness. Suddenly, a dim pinhole of light broke into the void. It began to grow, filling the darkness as dawn would creep over a landscape. I covered my eyes, shielding them from the brilliance.

A powerfully fragrant breeze blew in my direction. It smelled like incense or myrrh. It was soft, comforting, and familiar. I could smell the lavender my mother placed on my sheets as a child and the fields of grass I would run in after primary school. I smelled piping hot Earl Grey tea my mother made with milk and her signature cinnamon cakes that accompanied it. Every scent I'd ever loved was present. I knew someone was coming for me and I no longer feared anything—I no longer felt alone.

I felt compelled to walk closer to the light. Somehow, I knew everything I needed, everything I longed for, was in that light. I knew someone was waiting for me; I just needed to get there, but… I could not move. I was stuck. I willed every bit of power my body and mind could muster to lift my foot, but nothing happened.

"I can't get there! I'm trying but I can't make it!" I vocalized my predicament because I just knew someone was listening. Something in my heart told me that the person who was listening was the only one who could help me. Still, I could not move.

I looked to my left and there were hundreds of people moving forward toward the light. I looked to my right and there were hundreds more moving forward. I panicked. I yelled and cursed at them. Why could they move when I could not? I tried everything to get their attention, but their eyes were transfixed on the light ahead. Many closed their eyes and confidently walked forward. Their heads held high and backs fully erect. Some had tears of joy, but everyone had a smile. They all seemed to have a shared understanding of where they were going. I watched them disappear, one by one, as they reached the light's origin. They all looked at peace and unafraid.

On their faces, they wore the calm demeanors of men who had learned that their longest held beliefs had just been confirmed. I stood and watched each one enter the light. I'm not sure how long I stood there, but I anxiously waited until the end, thinking, "Maybe I'm last. Yes! That's it! I just had to wait my turn. My turn was coming." But my turn never came. When the final figure vanished, the light blinked out of existence, and darkness surrounded me once more.

I glanced around me, noticing that there were others who remained; like me, they had been left behind. I could hear people crying hysterically, cursing, yelling, and screaming.

"LET ME OUT OF HERE NOW!" I heard a man near me demand.

"Do you know who I AM?" He proclaimed.

Others began to take a cue from him and demanded to be heard as well. I guess they wanted to speak to management.

They all started yelling their names, credentials, and their achievements. *I'm Dr. So-and-so*, or *I'm on the board of this*. Somehow there must have been a mistake and they should be freed. While I agreed, I understood that no longer mattered. It seemed obvious that all the things that used to put us to the front of the line, did not work here.

Suddenly, their faces were illuminated in a bizarre red glow. Turning toward the source, I could make out a hole in the distance that had not been there before. We could finally see each other. There must have been hundreds of thousands of us scattered everywhere. We looked at each other and I immediately had a sense of shame. Many started running. A man beside me bolted in the other direction and shoved several people as he ran. Others tried to find a place to hide. But most fell to their knees. I just stood there—frozen.

If any of us didn't know what was going on or had been lying to ourselves about what was going on, or hoping our circumstances would change, we all knew time was up.

Another glowing red light came from a giant hole in the ground off in the distance. A stampede started. Everyone began to run away from the hole. People clawed and stomped on each other—each person fighting to get ahead of the other, but still having no idea where to go. A strong force began to aggressively pull me and others closer.

A feeling of terror filled me. The shock of everything that had kept me emotionless completely wore off. I struggled to resist the pull, but it felt like a thousand horses dragging me in the other direction. The pull became stronger as I saw others sucked into the hole screaming, "HELP ME!"

I was pulled over the edge, free falling. As my skin began to bubble and burst, I cried out among millions crying out. But my voice did not matter. My suffering did not matter. No one cared.

I could see a dark spiky surface approaching. I hit the ground with a sickening crunch feeling every bone in my body crack in the same instant. For a long time, I simply laid there feeling every nerve in my body catch fire. I had no concept of time passing. Was it days? Years? Eons? Why was this happening? When would it end? Why me?

*"And do not fear those who kill the body but cannot kill the soul. Rather fear him who can destroy both soul and body in hell." Matthew 10:28*

# Chapter Two

## The Truth

Jade's skin blistered from the intense heat, every pore on his worn body seeped blood. His torso twisted one hundred and eighty degrees as his bubbling skin melted off the muscles grafting his body to thorny ground. He fantasized about ending his suffering but understood there was no end.

Sometime ago, though, in a place like this, time is irrelevant, a thorn had grown into his eye, the pain was excruciating. There were moments when he screamed so loud, and for so long, it stripped the flesh on his throat raw and his blood flowed freely. In other moments he fell silent, unable to find the strength to even moan. What was the point? No one listening would come to save him, and those who were, only revelled in his misery. Others had given up completely, but Jade continually struggled for that one ounce of control. He was able to rip his arm free from the ground, but a strange force put it back. He cried, but no tears welled in his eyes. And though his body ached the familiar ache of sorrow, no water would surface and grace his cheeks giving him the slightest relief from the sweltering heat. Flashcard memories flipped through Jade's mind at every waking moment. Every formulating thought is about how he got there and the thoughts are the most painful. He now sees where he went wrong.

Any time happiness comes to mind, worms with razor sharp teeth crawl through his body and begin feasting on his organs. The glimpse is sometimes worth the pain, but it gives him no feeling of peace. In this place, he can never achieve serenity.

As the painful thoughts lingered in his mind, a giant beast with shaggy, matted brown hair, horns like a ram, six large black eyes, and fangs that jutted out of its mouth walked up to Jade exhaling its rotting breath. The beast's deep voice echoed through his body, "What's your name?"

"I am Jade."

"You've been summoned."

Without hesitation, the beast extracted his claws and dug them into Jade's throat. Blood gurgled in his mouth and pooled around the beast's claws. The beast ripped Jade's body off the ground, threw him over his slimy shoulder, and proceeded to walk across the thorny soil. Jade winced at each step.

Jade's eye scanned his surroundings for the first time since he had arrived. There were countless people being subjected to all manner of tortuous punishments. There were holes above. Every few minutes the holes vomited piles of people. Groups of beasts waited around the piles and ripped and bludgeoned through them as they laughed. Some beasts began violently raping anyone they could grab. The air was filled with a cacophony of weeping, moans, gnashing of teeth, and blood-curdling screams.

Jade could hear the sound of skulls cracking as they walked. The beast carried Jade over fiery plains and searing mountains, until finally they reached a fortress unlike anything Jade had ever seen or could imagine.

There was a towering black iron door protected by two beasts. The three began speaking a language Jade could not understand. The doors slowly opened to reveal a long bridge over a moat filled with blood and ligaments. As they crossed, Jade saw eyeballs still moving although separated from the sockets. There were half-eaten bodies and huge piranha-like creatures continually feasting.

When they finally reached the opened door, it revealed a long dark hallway. The floor was a gleaming void of black marble, and the walls were lined with an endless assortment of treasures and jewels from every major period in earth's history. Jade recognized some of the artifacts, but noticed they were not as they should be. At first glance they were beautiful, but upon looking closer, small details had changed. They all had a satanic element which made them frightening.

Jade noticed symbols he had seen before on currency and in art, which when he was alive seemed to have no meaning. He now realized they did have deep meaning. Enormous mirrors, stretching from floor to ceiling, with fancy frames engraved with intricate designs, lined the walls. They sparkled with gold, diamonds, and other exotic stones. There were so many reflections, doors and hallways; Jade assumed it would have been easy to lose one's way.

The beast finally deposited Jade in a dimly lit room. There were beaten, maimed, and hideous-looking bodies seated at an unfathomably long table. They stared at their empty plates, heads lowered, and gazes unwavering. Huge reptilian monsters that stood approximately nine feet tall entered the room and took seats at the table. They growled—intimidating all who were seated. We waited and waited. Then he appeared: Satan, in human form.

He was beautiful. The most handsome man Jade had ever seen. He walked in slow-motion, time seeming to crawl as he strode up to the table. He stopped abruptly, and everyone focused their attention on him.

"All eyes on me, exactly how I like it." Satan said. His voice was smooth and rhythmic.

He requested a glass of water and slid it down the long table. There was a short pause. Jade glanced around the table, and immediately five of the guests jumped for it and began fighting like rabid animals. Satan snapped his fingers and beasts grabbed each one and tossed them into a pit of fire.

"For those of you who do not know who I am… I have many names." The silence in the room was a sharp contrast to the horrific noise that Jade witnessed just beyond the walls. It was so quiet one could hear a pin drop.

Satan stood, "I take many forms…" he transformed himself into a beautiful woman, a cat, a snake, and then into his true form: a beast. He grew taller and larger than the other beasts, opened his mouth and roared. His breath created wind which enveloped the room and blew a few out of their seats. His claws were extremely long. He had short red hair all over his body and his eyes were solid black.

"Let me save you the suspense. You all have been chosen to return to the world—my world." He said.

Each guest looked at each other uncertain of what this meant. Were they getting a second chance? Could they start all over? Then Satan sat down and transformed himself back to his original form, and the other monsters followed suit.

Satan told the guests to stand in front of a mirror. Instantly, an image of them as they were on earth appeared. They were happy, healthy, and whole again. They began touching their bodies to see if they had actually changed into the images they were viewing. Jade marveled at how green his eyes were. He had forgotten.

"You can have all of this again." Satan said.

The images vanished and the mirror revealed their true appearances. A beautiful woman stood-up and began to speak.

"You have been selected to become soldiers in the dark army. Your charge is to collect as many human souls as you can while stationed on earth. The more souls you collect, the longer your stay will be. When you return, you will have a higher rank in hell."

"Are there any questions?" Satan asked. The guests were fearful and hesitant, but Jade needed clarity. "Are we being sent to earth to kill people?"

Satan and his cronies began to laugh. "You stupid souls always amaze me with how little you know. You idiots truly know nothing. You cannot actually kill a human… there are some rules. Unfortunately, only *He* has the power to take human life because *He* created human life. But, humans have the power to kill themselves, or other humans… this is where we work." Satan's laughter dwindled, and he began staring in deep thought.

He stood up abruptly, "If I had the power to murder every human, I would wipe the earth clean with their blood! None of them deserve to live. They should all burn in Hell!"

He started roaring, howling, and breaking whatever was around him. Another guest began to speak.

"So… How do we acquire souls then?"

Satan stopped in his tracks, breathing heavily, "What did you say?" he snapped.

Everyone, except the guests, knew that Satan went on wild tangents and had fits of anger that lasted for quite some time. No one dared interrupt him. Everyone had to sit and listen to his hate speech for as long as it lasted.

The guest became increasingly more nervous.

"I just wanted to understand, how we could collect souls if we could not kill them."

"NO, NO, NO! You interrupted me while I was speaking! This is my realm. *I* reign. *I* have no God—no master. I am GOD! You are just a stupid, worthless, soul that is here for ME to torture!" Satan barked.

Satan lifted him out of the chair, pinned him to the wall and summoned other demons to claw away at his body. The other guests cringed as they watched the mutilation.

Satan sat down at the head of the table and spoke again calmly.

"So, where was I? Ah, yes! The rules. We will train you in the dark arts, magic, esoteric knowledge, honing power from me, and most importantly, persuasion. While we cannot kill humans, there really is no need. If given enough time, enough opportunity, humans will certainly kill themselves."

The guests listened closely, now aware of how they had been deceived. Satan looked at them and began grinning.

"I'm sure you're surprised that I exist..." Satan watched their reactions. He enjoyed bringing this monumental oversight to their attention.

Jade lowered his head in shame as Satan broke out in hysterical laughter.

"See how utterly stupid you creatures are?" The Dark Master got up from his seat and smacked each guest over the head as he walked down the isle. "These idiots are so pathetic! And this... this is what God *loves*, supremely? These morons are who *He* bestowed free will upon? The thought sickens me!" Satan said.

Satan's laughter soon became extremely agitated. "They appreciate nothing they are given! You create them, and still they choose ME." He toppled over in laughter. Like a child, he rolled around on the floor barely able to catch his breath from gut-wrenching laughter. "That is why I knew I could get MORE souls than Him! I knew it! I am so much smarter than HIM!"

He rose from the floor and transformed himself over and over again into the most beautiful objects, animals, and humans. He kept repeating, "I am great, I'm better than the Father!" He kept repeating it as though repetition would somehow make it true. Everyone watched afraid to react. The guests and the monsters were not sure whether to laugh with him or to stay perfectly still. He was creative when it came to torture. No one could predict what was next, and that alone was terrifying.

He continued on his rant and called three naked women with chains around their necks, a man, and one of the monsters. He dragged them into a dark room and slammed the door. The guests stayed silent as they heard crying and screaming from the next room.

One of the monsters stood up and spoke. "To finish what the Dark Prince was saying, there are many ways to kill humans without actually 'killing' them. More than black magic, the powers of persuasion and distraction are the best tools in our arsenal. You were sent to hell because you did not believe in God, and you certainly did not believe Satan existed. This was not happenstance. Someone or something convinced you this was true and distracted you long enough to keep you from seeking the truth. You were fooled. This time, you will be returning to earth with full awareness of what is happening around you. However, your fate is sealed; your soul, the form that you have now, is tied to, and owned by Satan. After you acquire knowledge of the dark arts and learn how to harness power from Satan, you will become a demon. You will no longer have any resemblance to your old human form, however, you will be able to transform and give the appearance of a human in order to walk amongst them. Satan will determine how long you stay on earth. If you are doing a good job of acquiring souls, he will allow you to stay longer. When you return to hell, your rank will be higher and you will be servicing the Dark Prince. You will become more than just a tormented soul."

*"More than just a tormented soul?"* Jade pondered. What did that mean? Would the souls become like the slovenly beast that brought him to Satan's chambers? Or like the beasts roaming around continually tormenting souls? If so, their fates weren't any better – they were just slaves to Satan exacting his punishments for eternity.

The souls were reflective as the monster, now understood to be a ranking official, elaborated on the technicalities of getting back to earth.

"We use the dark arts to enter the world. Again, this annoying concept of 'Free Will' is the nonsense we have to circumvent. We cannot actually enter the world unless given permission to do so by a human. Satan is the only one who could do that. If humans want to communicate with us, they must use the dark arts to summon us, and then we can enter. One of the oldest and best tools is an Ouija board. But over time, we have devised thousands of other ways. The key is to "open the spirit." You can do this by gradually weakening the spirit over time. Subliminal messaging has worked wonders. We have been priming people to accept us for decades. TV and the internet have helped our message grow easily. Thankfully, this is a time in earth's history when almost anything a person does is tolerated and even accepted by their peers. There is no shame anymore. We have so many humans using the dark arts and opening their spirit; it is effortless for us to get to earth. Once their minds are open to us, we can use whatever tool we need to convince them to bring us into the world. Since Satan planted the first seed in the Garden, it has become easier and easier to acquire souls. Most times, humans do the work themselves."

Jade now had a better understanding of the goal but was still not completely sure about how this goal was achieved. He thought about his own life and could not remember a demon ever coming to him in the middle of the night and having him sign his name in blood, like the transaction is often portrayed. He could not even remember any definable moment when he could tell that his soul was "sealed" to the devil. So, he asked, "But how do we *get a hold of* the souls?"

The official sat down and spoke to them candidly.

"All you have to do is get a human to pledge his allegiance to the devil..."

Now, Jade was very confused and questioned whether his presence in hell may have been a mistake! He never used the words, *"I pledge my allegiance to Satan!"*

As if the official read Jade's thoughts he asked, "I bet you are thinking you never used those words, right?"

The souls nodded in agreement.

"Because you do not have to..." the official replied.

"As I stated before, being sent to Hell is a series of choices. Every choice you make either pushes you closer to Heaven or closer to Hell. One day a man can wake up and completely be aligned with Satan, because every choice he made was never for the greater good, it was always to advance his interests. Motivated by greed, lust, pride, gluttony, sloth, envy, or vengeance, you make the conscious decision that everything is about you. That is when you CHOSE to separate yourself from others and most importantly, become too prideful to even ask God for forgiveness. That is when your soul is aligned with the devil and that is our goal for humanity."

Hearing the truth was unbearable for Jade. If he were able to cry, tears would never stop. For the longest time, while he laid in torment, for some reason, he could not think of God. The thought of God never entered his mind, but ironically, in Satan's palace, in the middle of Hell, God is the perpetual topic of discussion. How to conquer Him is all that Satan ponders. God was real.

Consequently, more than the pain he'd experienced since he had been there; what hurt most was realizing that even the thought of God was a source of comfort, and the damned were incapable of thinking about God on their own. He knew now that the worst part of Hell was not the fire, brimstone, or the worms; it was the complete and utter separation from God. Just then, Satan walked out of the room soaked in blood and smiling as he spun the decapitated head of a girl on his finger.

"Are you all motivated now?" Satan asked.

***

As time passed, Jade's sadness quickly faded and he could only muster up feelings of hate and revenge. He now hated humans for having a chance at salvation. A chance he envied. He decided then, that he would do the work of Satan and direct all his hate toward the living. He now would do anything to see the demise of mankind.

*"Beloved, do not believe every spirit, but test the spirits to see whether they are from God, for many false prophets have gone out into the world." 1 John 4:1*

# Chapter Three

## Back to Earth

It was a day like any other in the Kingdom. You could smell peace and joy. These were not just feelings, but entities that filled every sense. These emotions had a taste, a sound, a feeling, and a look. There was an overwhelming feeling of comfort and satisfaction. The word "want" did not exist in heaven, because there was nothing imaginable to want. A soul had everything it could possibly desire and need. The only sounds are the ones of laughter and music in perfect harmony with each other. Children can be seen running and playing everywhere. Babies crawl around freely, and you might even catch glimpses of souls resting on clouds.

In heaven, there are souls and there are angels. The angels are soldiers in God's heavenly army charged with the duty of protecting His most prized creations: humans. God affords every soul the opportunity to become an angel, which is the highest honor in heaven. Being an angel is the opportunity to pay God back for all He has given. All souls must earn their wings before they can become angels, and a soul can be called at any time.

Steven was playing in the clear blue lake with a few children and an angel named Josiah. Josiah and Steven were wrestling in the water as the children laughed. Steven felt gentle warmth on his back. He turned around and called out, "Father?" God responded, "Yes, my son." He smiled and the other children started yelling, "Hi, Father!" with excitement in their voices. Instantly, they all felt a hug warm them.

"Steven, may I speak with you?" God asked.

Steven and Josiah gave each other a look, and Josiah whispered, "This is it…"

Steven responded, "Of course!" as he quickly jumped out of the lake and brushed himself off. Steven felt his body rise as he was gently lifted by doves. He was slowly released in a bright hallway before a throne. Jesus walked out and placed his arm lovingly around his shoulders, "You really enjoy the lake?" Jesus laughed.

Steven responded, "You know I love swimming!"

"The lake is there for you my brother; I knew you would love it." Jesus patted Steven on the back and took a seat at the right hand of the Father. God began to speak.

"Steven, I have called you today because I feel you are ready to earn your wings."

Steven fell to his knees and began crying tears of joy.

"Thank you, Father! Thank you so much for this opportunity!"

God continued, "There is a process to earning your wings, my son. The process is very trying and is not for the faint of heart."

Steven had a very basic understanding of the "process" from conversations with Josiah. He knew he would be sent back to earth; however, he also knew that every test was different and most importantly, not every soul passes.

"You will be sent back to earth to directly intervene in the life of one of my children. Many of my children are lost and need me. A child of mine, Sarah Michel, has been removed from me for some time now. She is approaching a critical time in her life where a decision she makes will leave her lost forever and it will impact the lives of many. If she makes the wrong choice, she will be cast down into the fire. You must guide her back to me."

Steven was doubtful of his ability and unsure of an approach.

"Father, how will I do that? What if she does not listen?" Steven asked.

"My child, she will not listen with her ears, but her heart is still slightly open. She has developed a tough and shrewd exterior from a hard life and the bad decisions of others." God said.

Jesus interjected, "Father, if I may..." God nodded in approval for Jesus to continue.

"Sarah spoke to me many years ago after a car accident. She pleaded for me to give her something that was lost and she could no longer have. But like many of my brothers and sisters, she asked for what she wanted and not what see needed. When she did not receive what she wanted, she lost her faith and has not spoken to me since. She is approaching a time in her life when she can no longer do it on her own." Jesus said.

Steven looked saddened and God knew there was still a choice for him to make.

"My child, you have been removed from the ills of the earth for so long. This task will not be easy and there are no guarantees. If this is not the type of service you would like to pursue, I understand and will always love you." God said reassuringly. Still, Steven was determined.

"No, Father. I want to help her, and I want to help you!" Steven said.

Jesus went on to explain the risks involved with this mission. He warned Steven that saving her soul will be a battle between good and evil. Once he entered the realm of earth, he could feel pain again, and he would be human. While back on earth, he would be susceptible to earthly temptations. Steven was advised to be in constant contact with the Father and the Son, so he would always remember his calling. God explained that the moment Steven could no longer hear Jesus' voice when praying he would become lost, and must work to find Him again. Steven would be on earth as long as it took for Sarah's heart to change one way or another. Steven understood the severity of his assignment, and for the first time, he became fearful and doubtful.

"Remember… I am always with you." Jesus said.

Steven understood he would become human, which meant that once again he would be in the most vulnerable state. He would have no powers of an angel and could not battle a demon on his own and win. The only advantage he had was the ability to recognize a demon without the demon being aware that he had already achieved salvation.

Should Steven show any sign of a deeper awareness of the spiritual realms, a demon would create every situation imaginable to force him to his own demise. Most importantly, Steven realized that every moment he was on earth he risked losing his own salvation. Once he could no longer hear the voice of God, the only advantage he had would no longer exist. Demons would become unrecognizable to him. If at any point he could not hear the voice of God and was killed, there was a chance he could be sent to Hell.

Jesus looked at Steven and knew everything that was weighing on his mind. Steven gazed back at Jesus and accepted his mission.

*"Let us not become conceited, provoking one another, envying one another."*
*Galatians 5:26*

# Chapter Four

## Sarah

Her eyes opened and were transfixed on the thing ahead. "I should probably call someone about that soon." She uttered.

The small crack in the ceiling had grown longer since she first saw it. Her alarm progressively grew louder, but she ignored it and continued to lay there. It had become increasingly more difficult to get up every morning. There were some days, if not for her career, she would probably stay in bed watching the crack in the ceiling.

Sarah grabbed her phone and quickly scanned each new email. Luckily, there were no missed calls from work, so the emails could wait until she reached the office. She smacked the alarm button hard and grabbed the remote. It may have been reflexive at this point because her fingers instinctively found CNN.

The volume was loud—it had to be loud. For Sarah, the scripted banter of news anchors was a comical paradox. They could never transition appropriately between stories—most still smiling as they delivered sobering news. How does one shift from viral videos of cats playing keyboards to bombings in Syria?

Sarah slid her pedicured toes into her slippers, threw her satin robe over her shoulders and made her way toward the kitchen. She could smell the imported Columbian coffee before it brewed. An ex-boyfriend once told her, "A cup of coffee is the only guaranteed bit of happiness you can count on." That turned out to be true, because she couldn't count on him.

She entered the bathroom and turned the faucet until it couldn't go any further and aggressively doused her face in cold water. The sound of rushing water as it pooled at the basin of the sink reminded her of childhood. Her father would often pretend he was going to spray her with water while he gardened, but never did. It became a joke between them that lasted late into her teens—just before he died.

She reached for a washcloth to gently dry her face and slowly opened her eyes. Confronted by her reflection, she really saw herself. Her real hair was splitting at the ends from too much straightening and her roots had grown out. It was time for a touch up. Her natural chestnut-brown coloring was a sharp contrast to the dirty blonde highlights she adored. She'd almost forgotten how her eyes looked without greenish-blue contacts. They seemed darker than she remembered.

All the background noise began to fade. The news anchors were no longer audible. The rushing water muted. There was total silence. An intense unexplainable feeling of sadness shrouded her. Sarah tried desperately not to cry, but knew that was the only acceptable time for it. So she did.

She dropped to the floor and pushed herself to the nearest wall. She held her knees tight against her chest and hugged herself. She wanted to cry out to someone or something. There was something she needed, but could not articulate.

Sarah was always confused at this exact moment, and was ill equipped to solve this problem. She was never good with feelings, and not understanding why she felt this way inexplicably made her angry and frustrated. She released a deep sigh and then quickly composed herself.

"I might need a stronger dosage of Zoloft." She thought.

Each morning was a continual battle to keep it together—keep from breaking apart. Sarah turned her head rapidly and faced the far corner of the bathroom. She stared at the empty space momentarily. Nothing was there. She felt silly expecting to see someone standing there. Sarah pushed herself off the ground and wiped her eyes. She glanced one more time at the mirror, disrobed, and stepped in the shower.

***

Sarah started to love gray. Her closet looked like a monochromatic grayscale devoid of black or white. She never really liked black or white. For her the colors were so "here" or "there" when gray was contentedly in the middle.

Her closet was neat. Her clothes were freshly dry-cleaned and lined up perfectly. She needed a pantsuit. She was feeling particularly venomous today so she grabbed her Louis Vuitton snake-skinned pumps with tote bag to match. No outfit was complete without Gucci sunglasses.

She walked confidently into the lobby and heads turned. She stepped outside and waited under the canopy. The concierge greeted her cheerfully.

"Good morning, Ms. Michel, how are you?"

Sarah, more concerned with locating gloves in her oversized bag, didn't respond.

"It's unusually cold today."

"What?"

"Oh, I said it's unusually—"

"Why am I waiting out here?" Sarah interjected. "Shouldn't there be a car here *waiting* for me?"

"Ah yes, Ms. Michel, you're right, but you were about thirty minutes behind, and I wasn't sure if you were heading to the office today. Your car was assigned to another resident—but another car will be here shortly."

Sarah pulled her sunglasses down to see what was written on his name tag.

"Anthony?"

"Yes, ma'am!" He responded.

"How long have you been working here?"

Sarah sounded less annoyed and seemed genuinely interested in knowing.

"I've been here for three years—around the time you moved in."

"Really? I thought you were a new hire."

Anthony was confused once he realized she had no recollection of him. He greeted her every morning for three years.

"No ma'am, I'm here every morning."

Sarah may not have noticed him because she was always on her phone or simply preoccupied with something else. Whatever the reason for missing him all these years, it was forgiven. Anthony just appreciated the dialogue.

"You like it here?" Sarah asked. She was subtly flirtatious, carefully looking him over as she waited for his response.

Anthony couldn't hide his grin. He'd had a small crush on Sarah since the first time he saw her, but never thought he had a chance. He still didn't think he had one, but acknowledgment from a beautiful woman was enough for him.

"I do like it here. Everyone has been friendly, and my supervisors are always willing to help… and answer any questions I have."

Sarah was bored and made no effort to conceal it. She scrolled through Facebook as Anthony spoke. Aware he was starting to lose her, but eager to continue the conversation, he inquired about her interests.

"So… what do you do for work? You always seem so busy. It must be important."

"It is important—very important. It requires A LOT more

thought than opening doors for people. Which is why I'm surprised I'm still waiting for my car!"

Anthony got the subtle dig and was surprised at how quickly her tone changed.

Sarah was done feigning interest. She was done chatting with "the help." She was ready to go.

"It should be here any moment now." Anthony said.

"Listen, when I come outside I just want to be able to hop in my car and go, understand? So, if I'm late, pick up that little phone and ask—don't assume—what my morning plans are."

Anthony's smile faded, "You're absolutely right, Ms. Michel. I'll make sure to do as you've requested in the future."

The car pulled up and Anthony opened the door. Sarah stepped in; once seated, she rolled down the window.

"I hope I was clear… I really wouldn't want to get your supervisor involved."

Someone had to teach these people professionalism. In her experience, they were quick to talk and slow to perform. Sarah has always been at the top of her game and expected others to do the same. No one made concessions for her, and she didn't want any. She arrived earlier than most and always was the last to leave. She worked through college, interned, fetched coffee, and took a lot of crap from people to enjoy a six-figure salary.

Sarah learned that people don't become successful in Washington, D.C.—the political hub of the world—by being pushovers, or waiting their turn. You want something? Take it. Better yet, convince someone to give it to you.

Her company was one of the biggest names in government contracting in the nation. The company did billion-dollar business with the government because it always anticipated the needs of agencies like the Department of Defense, Central Intelligence, and others. It had a sizable portfolio of investments and her firm was frequently looking to expand, acquire, or find the latest innovations. Sarah climbed the corporate ladder by being shrewd. She willingly made the decisions many hesitated to make, and for that, she won respect in an industry dominated by men.

When Sarah arrived at the office, her assistant was there to greet her.

"Good morning Ms. Michel! Here is your double-shot skim-latte and low-fat bran muffin."

Sarah passed her and made no effort to grab the items. Instead, sat in her office and waited to be served.

"Who called me, Sally?"

Her assistant's name was actually Shiloh, but Sarah didn't think she looked like a Shiloh and thought "Sally" was a better fit.

Her assistant handed Sarah a spreadsheet of all the incoming calls that morning with the name, time, date, and nature of the call. Sarah found this to be another teachable moment about "being at the top of your game."

"Sally, I need the number for Capt. Edward Holland." Sarah said authoritatively.

Shiloh looked puzzled.

"I'm sorry Ms. Michel… did I forget to place the number on the sheet?"

Sarah balled the sheet up, threw it across the room, leaned forward and stared at her.

"No… his number is on the spreadsheet. However, I asked *you* for the number, Sally."

Shiloh, clearly intimidated, stumbled over her words.

"Ah… umm… well, Ms. Michel… I don't have the number memorized…" Shiloh replied, wondering what the penalty would be for this infraction.

Sarah began looking at her computer screen and typed as she spoke.

"One of the criteria I was insistent upon when Human Resources interviewed candidates for your position, Sally, was that they select someone smart—with a good memory. Though your position does not require much thought, I was adamant on that point."

Shiloh nodded to show her understanding.

"You might not have realized this, but our company has supported his program's office for over a decade. We have about a dozen other loyal clients like him that specifically work with me because of the relationship we've built. If you are going to assist me, you need to know them as well as I do. You need to know everything about them—including their numbers—by heart. I want you to embed this information into your memory." Sarah said.

Sarah knew this was never communicated to Shiloh before and was also aware the expectation was unreasonable. However, she wanted to see her reaction. She wanted to see if she'd be challenged.

"Is there anything else I can get for you, Ms. Michel?"

Sarah looked up from her computer screen annoyed by how spineless Shiloh was.

"No, I'm done with you." Sarah replied.

Shiloh lowered her head and closed the door.

Sarah was a bit behind that morning; she needed to make a few phone calls before the 10:00 A.M. meeting. Ronald Henry's retirement party happened last week, and the Senior Management position was now open in the Acquisitions Department.

Ron was a great mentor and told her that when the position opened, she would be a prime candidate. Her portfolio was proof enough. In three years, through her direct effort, the company acquired land, rental property throughout the District, oil refineries, and was making more money than they knew what to do with.

Sarah knew she couldn't ride on those accolades forever. In this business she was only as good as her last big idea. Her competition was, David Mercer, the son of a close family friend to a board member.

Ever since he started working for the company she hated him. He came out of Yale and was placed in a junior management position with no real experience. The company needed to fill the position right away; instead, the position was held for three months because David was vacationing in Madrid. Meanwhile, Sarah juggled the job duties of two managers for three months.

When David arrived, he acted like he was her boss. He made demands masked with the question, "May I ask for your assistance on something urgent?" If it were anyone else he would have been made aware of her seniority in the company and disregarded without a second thought, but he was protected.

The President of the company entered Sarah's office late one evening—a day before David was to arrive, and said: "As you know, David starts tomorrow. Make sure you make him feel at home and provide him with the assistance he needs to become a star like you."

Sarah knew they favored David and if she wanted a chance at the position, she had to at least pretend to be a team player.

Sarah was about to walk out of her office to the meeting when her assistant popped in.

"Your meeting is in the Executive Boardroom in five minutes. Oh! And Dr. Bailey called, his number is: (202) 513-5554."

Sarah looked at her and shook her head.

"I am heading there now… I will call back." She said.

Sarah snatched the pen and the legal pad her assistant had ready and marched down the hall.

David and Sarah arrived at the entrance of the Executive Boardroom at the same time. David greeted her with a smile.

"How are you this morning?" he said as he held the door open.

Sarah flashed a quick smile and walked in before him. The President, the Vice President, the CFO, and board members were all seated. When David and Sarah walked in, the board members immediately started smiling and stood up to embrace him. Sarah had to pretend as though she was interested in the discussion the group was having. They asked David how he liked D.C. and the board kept stroking his ego by emphasizing the impression he made on the staff in the short time he had been with the company.

Sarah tried so hard to hide her envy, but it was nauseating. She had to take the focus off of him somehow.

"I'm sorry… is there an agenda for this meeting?"

The President replied, "Oh no, consider this meeting informal. We are business, but not all the time, Sarah."

"Of course!" she replied slightly embarrassed.

The President used the opportunity to transition to the purpose of the meeting.

"I've called you both here, because you are the young stars of this company. It is no secret that Ron's position needs to be filled. To be frank, you both are up for consideration." The President said.

David smiled and nudged Sarah. She flashed another fake smile and continued to be attentive as he spoke.

"You both have leadership qualities that are great assets for this position. David, though you have only been here for a few months, you've built excellent relationships with many overseas contacts and have really begun to formulate some truly innovative initiatives that I believe will lead us into the future. And, Sarah, you have definitely made the company money and maintained the consistency we need to stay vital. With that said, we will be evaluating your work performance for the next few months. Our proposal period is coming up. We all look forward to seeing where else you think this company should go."

David winked at Sarah then directed his comment to the President.

"I mean… would two stars be too bright?" David asked.

A few executives chuckled. David nudged Sarah for a second time. Annoyed, she cut her eyes at him and shifted the light hearted moment back to a serious tone.

"You won't be disappointed. I'll put us in the right place and prove I'm the best candidate for the position." Sarah said as she ignored David's ridiculous gestures.

The executives nodded, then stood-up and shook both their hands. Sarah quickly exited the boardroom and David hurried behind.

"Hey, hey…, you walk so fast!" David said jokingly as he pursued her.

"Yes. I walk fast because I have work to do and things to accomplish during the day. Unfortunately, I don't have the luxury of chatting and making small talk with family friends." Sarah turned toward him and stopped abruptly. David almost ran into her. Slightly aggravated, Sarah asked, "So, what can I help you with David?"

David smiled and began to speak. He was a tall, good looking guy, and Sarah could tell that his smile had gotten him places in life. He had a charming relaxed demeanor that most people gravitated towards.

"Well, what I proposed in the meeting was not intended to be a joke, even though I think everyone took it that way." David said.

"What are you talking about?" Sarah replied making no attempt to hide her annoyance.

"When I asked if two stars would be too bright, I was implying that one position could in actuality be two." David said. "We are both knowledgeable, and I think we could serve the company better if we worked together."

Sarah took a step back and folded her arms.

"So… you're suggesting that we both become senior executives in the Mergers and Acquisitions Department…?"

David placed his arms behind his back and removed his smile to demonstrate his seriousness about the proposal.

"Yeah, I am." David said.

Sarah paused for a moment and laughed. How could he make such a proposition? He knew that he did not have what it took to be in a senior position and was suggesting a partnership just to mask his inadequacies. Sarah was not having it.

"Absolutely not! No way!" She said as she continued walking.

David followed Sarah into her office where he greeted her

assistant.

"Hey, Shiloh!"

Shiloh smiled almost blushing. Sarah glared at her assistant who quickly went back to an email.

"David why are you in here?" Sarah said as she took a seat.

"I just want you to think about it. That's all! To me, titles aren't as important as what we could accomplish as a team for the company. I have been working on a project that would be great if we shared our contacts. I think the proposal is good enough that the execs would consider us working together on this." David said.

Sarah thought about his proposal for a second, but cringed at the thought of her and David being at the *same* level after he had only been working for the company for seven months. The proposition was ridiculous!

"Sorry, David. I already have a very big project I am working on." Sarah replied casually.

David, unaffected by the rejection, shrugged his shoulders and smiled.

"No problem, then… best of luck to you." David replied as though he was assured a victory.

The truth was Sarah had no big project. The executives alluded to the fact that they wanted something cutting edge, and Sarah was in a bit of a rut. She was consistent but not innovative. She could not keep bringing the same thing to the table.

When David walked out, he left the door to Sarah's office slightly cracked. He was talking to her assistant.

"How did the test go?" David asked.

Shiloh, excited that he remembered, replied, "I got a 96 percent! Thank you so much for the books!"

"Anytime!" David said. "You have to join me and my intern, Jamal, for lunch today. We're going to check out that new sports bar in Chinatown."

"Great! That'll work for me." Shiloh said with a big smile.

"We'll meet you in the lobby around twelve." David winked at Shiloh and exited. Sarah called Shiloh into her office.

"Sally, could you get Dr. Bailey on the phone?"

"Sure!" Shiloh replied cheerfully. Sarah could tell that she was very happy about the lunch.

"Oh, Sally, one more thing…" Sarah stopped typing and looked up at her. "I hope you don't have any lunch plans, I'm really going to need you today."

Shiloh's smile faded and she closed the door. Sarah began breathing heavily and frantically searched for her anxiety medication when the phone rang. It was Dr. Bailey.

"I need to see you today. Do you have a slot this afternoon?" Sarah asked.

"Slow down Sarah. Yes, I do. Come around 3:30 PM." Dr. Bailey replied.

Sarah hung up the phone, placed her head in her hands, and then tapped her fingers on the desk as she thought about all she needed to tell her psychiatrist.

***

When Sarah arrived at Dr. Bailey's office, she had to wait for about 15 minutes to be seen. Her leg shook as she constantly checked the time.

"Dr. Bailey will see you now." The secretary said.

She stormed into the office and slammed the door.

"I absolutely hate him!" Sarah shouted, as though shouting was her only source of relief.

"Calm down Sarah, hate is such a strong word." Dr. Bailey said.

Dr. Bailey had been her psychiatrist for close to a decade; he knew her better than anyone.

"He literally makes me sick!" Sarah replied. "He has done nothing of significance with his life, yet he gets everything! Everyone loves him and thinks he is so smart and charming when I know he's not!"

Sarah took a seat on the couch, folded her arms, and

became reflective.

"You know what he asked me today?"

Dr. Bailey was startled by her sudden jolt forward. He calmly took a seat and signaled for her to continue.

"He had the audacity to ask me if we could work together on a project! Just so he can slack the hell off!" Sarah said.

"Maybe he respects you and your work and can see the two of you working well together. Have you considered that motive?" Dr. Bailey replied.

Sarah was offended by the suggestion he made, and quickly corrected him.

"No… that's not it, he wants to use me!"

Sarah got up and paced around the office. She glanced at Dr. Bailey scribbling in his notepad.

"I need to be on my 'A' game."

Dr. Bailey looked at her and wrote some more. Sarah walked closer and positioned herself right in front of him to get his attention.

"I need another prescription." Sarah said.

"Sarah, you're not due for a refill for at least a couple months. No, I will not give you a prescription." Dr. Bailey said with authority.

Sarah inched closer to him and began undoing her shirt.

"Come on Andrew, I know how to handle meds; I won't OD."

Dr. Bailey and Sarah began having a sexual relationship about five years ago. Their inappropriate and unhealthy relationship has been a series of temper tantrums and lies. They used each other to satisfy needs that never reached the root of the problem. Sarah made him feel young, and he rewarded her with drugs.

Sarah removed his glasses and passionately kissed him. Dr. Bailey reached over and turned down a picture of his wife and children. Sarah stopped kissing him and looked back at the frame now face-down on his desk. He slid her bra straps down and kissed her neck and shoulders.

"Why do you always do that?" Sarah asked.

She was irritated. Dr. Bailey was in the process of undoing her bra hoping to distract her.

"Why does it concern you?" he asked.

Sarah raised herself off of his lap abruptly ending the romance.

"Just stop the Psych bullshit!" She reached for her blouse. "You're never leaving her are you?" Sarah asked as she tried to maintain her composure. Dr. Bailey closed his eyes momentarily as he grabbed the back of her arm.

"Don't touch me!" She screamed.

Worried someone might hear, Dr. Bailey whispered, "Sarah, lower your voice!"

Sarah in an even louder tone replied, "Just give me the damn prescription, ASSHOLE!"

Dr. Bailey took a pen out of his pocket and gave her what she wanted. He just wanted Sarah to calm down and leave. She snatched the prescription, wiped her sleeve across her eyes and stormed out of his office.

***

Sarah arrived home, rested her back against the wall, and slid to the floor. She studied the furniture in the foyer. It was modern and sleek—beautiful, but uninviting. She began the usual routine: She set the TV to CNN, changed into her silk pajamas, and pulled out her laptop. The light blinked on her answering machine. She had a voicemail. Andrew probably called to apologize. She pressed the button and listened.

"Hi, sweetheart, it's your mother. I know I'm probably the last person you want to hear from, but… I love you. I need to make sure you're okay and doing well. Please call me."

Sarah pressed delete. She took one Xanex, reached under her bed and pulled out a bottle of Merlot. She poured a full glass and downed it quickly. Slightly buzzed, she slid under her gray comforter and drifted off to sleep.

*"Put on the whole armor of God that you may be able to stand against the schemes of the devil. For we do not wrestle against flesh and blood, but against the rulers, against the authorities, against the cosmic powers over this present darkness, against the spiritual forces of evil in the heavenly places." Ephesians 6:11 - 12*

# Chapter Five

## Training

Jade had been training for a while. There was no way for him to know how long, time is immeasurable when the backdrop is an eternity. There were about five hundred souls in groups of about fifty, each taking instructions from a demon. Some were practicing invisibility, others were learning how to transform, some had their eyes closed and looked like they were in deep meditation. Those souls were learning how to harness power from the devil.

Azul, was the instructing official of Jade's group. He seemed quieter and less angry compared to the others. He was odd. He was short, old, and balding. The other officials in Hell transformed themselves into the most splendid creatures, but Azul looked plain and boring. He had a blue hue to him and he wore glasses.

Jade concluded this must have been his appearance while

living. For Jade, that was the only rational explanation as to why he would choose to present himself in that manner.

"You're aware that you've been selected to return to earth." Azul said as he paced before them. "When you return, you will have power which must be developed extensively before it can be used. This power stems from masterfully controlled and focused hate." Azul said as his eyes swept the room for their reactions.

"The greater level of control you have, a higher level of mastery will be achieved when manipulating the dark arts. You will have the skill to execute so much more chaos."

Jade's attention was unwavering as he listened. Nothing was more important than what Azul was saying.

"At this moment, you are miserable tormented souls who can only feel regret, despair, and restlessness. You have the inability to experience any positive emotion; however, hate can disguise true feelings. Hate is so powerful; it is the one emotion besides love that can consume a soul."

Azul went on to explain that the embodiment of hate is Satan, and Satan would need to be used as a resource to develop their hateful powers.

"Hate on your own is not powerful enough. As a former human, hate is not a natural emotion but a learned one." Azul said.

Azul emphasized that the best demons hone in on what humans feel. The best demons understand human desires and then manipulate them. Azul made it clear that some humans were harder to manipulate than others.

"Do not make the mistake of thinking that all humans are weak." Azul said.

Confused, Jade asked, "Some humans have power as well?"

"No. They do not have 'power' but there are some humans that have an awareness of the spiritual realms—either because they truly believe without knowing and can feel it in their hearts, or they know definitively." Azul said.

Not satisfied with the explanation Azul gave, Jade prodded.

"How could people know definitively God exists or that Hell is real? If these people do know, it will be impossible to acquire their souls, they know the truth!"

Azul was slightly agitated by Jade's assumption and snapped.

"It is very possible! It can happen... It definitely can happen."

Azul described situations where some humans passed on and saw heaven, but were sent back to earth. He stressed that these humans are the most dangerous because they are trying to save souls. They are usually attempting to save the soul of a human who must make a decision that could affect the lives of many.

"These humans must be eliminated." Azul said. "A demon cannot tell who these humans are because they blend seamlessly into the population, but these humans can recognize evil."

Azul assured the group that if they paid close enough attention, they would be able to recognize them as well. Jade wanted to know more. Jade did not want anyone or anything shorting his stay on earth.

If Jade had to describe Hell, there would be no words in any language that completely convey the feelings of despair and immense agony he experienced at every moment. He did not want to be there.

"Most humans question and are curious because they do not know. This leads them to investigate. They have the desire to just take a peek. Once they have, they are already deeper than they'd planned to go, and before they know it, they're lost. On the other hand, humans that have seen the light will try their hardest to avoid temptation at all costs, because they know their frailties and also know everything that is at stake. This is the difference between humans who are aware and those who are not." Azul said.

The thought of this triggered something in Jade that made his eyes turn red. These "special" humans could impede his progress and send him back to Hell. The thought angered him, and he could feel heat rising within him. Just then a shot of fire flew from his hand and scorched the floor. Jade was surprised, uncertain what just happened.

The group of souls studied him cautiously, their expressions barely masking their fear. Azul nodded with approval and commented, "That is the power of hate… Now I will teach you how to control it."

The lessons went on and Azul's group continued to improve in their mastery of the dark arts. The souls had a basic level of mastery and their hate was growing every moment. Azul asked them to sit down and prepare for the most important lesson. It was the lesson of persuasion. Azul made two holographic images appear before the group.

"Does anyone know who these people are?" he asked.

One soul responded, "It's Adolf Hitler and Jim Jones, leader of Jonestown."

Azul nodded, "You are correct. They both sat at this very table and were given the same opportunity as you to return to earth. They used no black magic; they only used the power of persuasion. They convinced humans to kill each other and themselves. Much of the hate they conjured up is still embedded in the minds of people who follow their writings and their visions generations later." Azul said.

Azul could not stress the importance of understanding the nature of humans enough. He continued to use every opportunity to shape their understanding of this lesson.

"Ultimately, humans are designed for service; however the irony is that they must *choose* service. Why would humans *choose* to be servants when they are *free* to be kings? Why would humans choose to listen and obey when they can know it all themselves and create the rules? These are the questions we never answer for them. These are the desires mankind has wrestled with since the beginning of time. We encourage their natural instincts and desires that will inevitably lead them toward the wrong choice. We even encourage their intellect. Many times humans have 'thought' themselves out of salvation. Understanding their desires is the key to acquiring their souls."

Azul was in his element, the souls were captivated by the lesson.

"Humans want to be loved, want to be accepted, want comfort and security. For much of these things to be acquired there must be sacrifice. To be loved you must also love others, to be accepted, you must accept others; to have comfort and security; you must be content with what you have. But humans want quick fixes. Humans want these rewards without the work, the effort, or the sacrifice… And they are vain, so very vain! How can a human love another when his greatest love is of self? How can humans accept others when they constantly categorize and judge by the most insignificant things? How can a human be comfortable and secure with what he has, when his brother has more? This is where we come in. You see, they already desire these things. It is natural for them to do so, therefore, we just show them the short cuts. We show them the value of instant gratification. We emphasize the benefit of doing what feels good, while most importantly, making humans believe every problem can be solved on their own.

"But souls must be acquired swiftly once aligned with the devil. Every moment a human is alive, is a chance at redemption— a chance at salvation. That's a chance we can't afford." Azul said.

Azul went on to explain how demons could kill humans, and there were three ways a demon could kill. First, a demon could kill by using the power of persuasion and convincing humans to kill each other. Second, demons could possess a human soul and then have the power to commit murder while hosted in the body. However, Azul explained that this act took permission from the human to enter the soul and a great deal of energy once engaged. There was also an element of danger. If the word of God were to be spoken while a demon had entered a human spirit, the pain would be unbearable. The demon would die and return to Hell. Azul explained the final and best way to kill a human was to convince him to kill himself—suicide. Suicide meant a human lost hope, no longer had any faith, and believed the problem could be solved alone.

"Humans who commit suicide have no concept of a bigger plan and are so self-involved that their relationship with the world and others is no longer important." Azul said.

As the lessons continued, Jade began to notice strange and dramatic changes were happening within his body. His muscle mass was increasing, his hair was getting darker and more dense. He grew fangs. As each moment passed he became more like a beast. Azul also noticed this change. Jade was progressing much faster than the others. Misery and despair were hard emotions to overcome, but Jade somehow suppressed these emotions and filled himself with the hate needed to become demonic.

***

The day Jade had waited for arrived. It was time for each group to prove they were capable of passing into the world. All the souls were lined up; some looked more like souls and others looked more like demons. This was the only chance the students had.

One soul had very little hair on her body and still looked like a tormented soul. One of the officials asked her to transform into a dog. She did. Another official asked her to become invisible. She did. Then Satan created the illusion of a baby. The baby looked real as it crawled around crying as though it were looking for its mother.

"Kill the baby." Satan said.

The soul closed her eyes and tried focusing hard, but she could direct no hate toward the child. She strained and tried hard to kill the child, but she was unable to do it.

"Look at me…" Satan said.

The soul was petrified. Satan approached her and placed his finger on her chin titling her head toward him.

"You still have light in your eyes…" The soul quickly closed her eyes and continued to try to muster up the courage to kill the baby. But it was too late; Satan had already seen that she was weak. He removed the image of the baby and summoned Jade.

By this time Jade looked like a beast. He was about 8 ½ feet tall, had razor sharp claws, and absolutely no light in his eyes. The officials asked him to do almost every trick, and he did flawlessly. Everyone was impressed except Satan. Satan approached him and looked into his eyes; they both stared at each other for a long time. Satan could feel the hate. Satan pointed to the soul that went before him.

"I want you to torture her, but… be creative."

Jade looked at Satan and smiled. Suddenly, Jade had transformed himself into a baby and started crawling toward her. Jade smiled innocently, as a baby would, then his face turned gruesome and he began forcefully and violently head butting her until her skull caved in. The officials stood-up and clapped. Azul remained seated, seemingly unimpressed by the show. Satan leaned down and whispered in Azul's ear.

"To be so miserable and sad, you sure do train the best soldiers. You really should start to enjoy your stay here; this *is* where you wanted to be." Satan continued clapping for Jade, as Azul quietly exited the room. Jade noticed Azul leave down a dark hallway and followed.

"Azul, where are you going?" Jade asked.

"I am going to my dudgeon; you will be able to experience some happiness once you return to earth. Congratulations…" Azul said, as he continued to walk rapidly.

"Wait! I heard some things about you that make no sense. Satan never beats you? Everyone takes abuse from him no matter what their level. You train his best soldiers and have been given opportunities to return to earth several times, but you've declined. Why? Why are you always so sad? You do not have it half as bad as souls here!" Jade said angered that Azul rejected the opportunity he had just killed for.

Azul looked at Jade and his eyes began to water. Jade had never seen anyone's eyes water in Hell. Azul told Jade to follow.

When Azul opened the door to his dungeon, the room was

freezing. Colder than anything Jade had ever felt. It was so cold it burned.

"Do you know how I knew some humans were aware of God's existence?" Azul asked.

Jade shook his head.

"I knew Heaven existed because I had been there..." Azul uttered with a shaky voice.

Jade was flabbergasted. He could not hide the shock written on his face.

"You have been to Heaven? How did you end up here?"

Azul pushed his hand out toward Jade, silencing him.

"That is what I think about every moment... That is the only thing I think about." Azul said, as tears began flowing from his eyes.

"Satan mocks me and laughs at me! He whispers in my ear and says that I am just like him, because, like him, I chose to be here in Hell, rather than in Heaven after knowing and experiencing what Heaven is like."

Jade just watched Azul as his blank stare hit the floor.

"You are right. He does not abuse me because the thought of not being in Heaven after being there is torment enough! Instead of just letting me sit in solace, instead of letting me endure the misery and pain I brought on myself, he makes me train his soldiers. Why would I want to return to earth? So I could feel the grace of God again and become even more saddened to know that grace is not for me. I am damned." Azul said.

Azul's tears began to flow faster and heavier. His tears were ice cold.

Jade's curiosity encouraged him to simply ask, "What was Heaven like?" Suddenly Azul grew to a tremendous height, hovered over him and roared louder than any demon Jade ever heard. "GET OUT!"

Jade ran out of the room terrified. Once the door closed, Azul transformed back into his old form and began weeping uncontrollably. The ice that covered the walls in Azul's room was from an eternity of his tears.

***

Jade reached the final stage before returning to earth. He was now a demon. Jade looked around at the other demons that made it to this stage. Out of a group of about 500 souls, only 30 became demonic.

It was clear that becoming a demon really meant immersing oneself in a complete state of denial. Most souls were like Azul. They could not change their misery into hate because they now had complete awareness of who to blame for their suffering. It was neither God nor humans, but themselves.

It angered Satan that he could not flood the earth with demons. Even while reigning in Hell he was forced to abide by the rules of God. He still had boundaries and all the illusions he could conjure could not hide that one solitary truth. Satan had to be relentless and needed to work hard to build his army. Satan created support systems for his new demonic creations. He encouraged them to link with very well-connected demons living on earth for centuries.

"Jade, when you return to earth, go see Samuel Linden, he's expecting you." Satan told him.

Jade and the other newly trained demons were in the room of voices. This was the place where people on earth using Ouija boards and other methods of black magic communicated with demons. You could hear voices saying, "Enter our world dark lord." Many were chanting. The demons moved their hands in the air spelling out letters to communicate with them. Jade answered the call of a human named Max.

The demons were taught that before they could enter the world they needed the permission of a human. The demons also needed a blood sacrifice from earth to open a portal. Max had given Jade the permission he needed, but had difficulty catching something to kill.

"Max, do you have a domesticated animal?" Jade scribbled in the air.

The cursor on the Ouija board was moving fast. Max was writing as fast as he could trying to decipher the message.

"Yes." Max replied.

Jade wrote, "Kill the animal. Hurry, there is not much time."

Max jumped up and crept into his sister's room. Her cat, Mitzi, was sitting there. Max had some cat food that lured her to him. He entered his room and tied the cat's feet and arms and began chanting.

"I summon all the darkness to envelope this place and allow the dark lord to enter the realm of earth, the devil's domain."

Jade listened to his chant and wondered why it was taking so long. Why he had to be so dramatic. He quickly wrote, "Hurry!"

Max saw the cursor move and placed the cat on the board. He lifted his knife, hesitated, and then brought it down into the animal's furry abdomen. Max saw a portal open up on the floor. Wind blew violently in his room as posters of rappers and rock stars flew off the walls.

A vortex opened up before Jade. It was red and black. Without hesitation, Jade jumped in and was immediately swept away. The portal twisted and turned, he was moving as fast as light. Upon his arrival, Jade shot up, hit the ceiling in Max's room and landed on the floor. Max, pressed himself against the door in fear. Jade was lying in the fetal position naked. He was in human form again. Max cautiously approached Jade and slowly knelt beside him.

"Water… get me water." Jade's parched voice uttered.

Max ran downstairs and got water from the kitchen. When he returned, Jade was lying on his back. Max gently put the water to his lips as he sipped. The cool water down Jade's throat felt so good. He opened his eyes and Max was hovered over him.

Max smiled, "It worked! It worked, you are here dark lord." Though Jade was very weak, the few sips of water gave him enough energy to stand. Jade found a mirror and looked at himself. He touched his face and his body.

He was beautiful again. He was not bleeding; he felt no pain. He smiled. "I am here on earth. I am here!" he bellowed.

He hugged Max and the happiness he felt gave him enough energy to lift Max up and spin him around. He could laugh again for the first time in a long while. Jade closed his eyes and whispered, "I am back."

*"And we know that for those who love God all things work together for good, for those who are called according to his purpose." Romans 8:28*

# Chapter Six

## The Way

Josiah and Steven rested in the green pastures of Heaven. Steven turned and looked at Josiah.

"I accepted my mission…" Steven said.

Josiah smiled and nodded.

"I knew you would, my brother" Josiah replied. "There is no higher honor than to accept the mission bestowed upon you by the Most High."

"I know and I am appreciative. But—I am scared." Steven said truthfully.

Josiah sighed and closed his eyes. Steven knew that Josiah understood his concern but could also offer no further words of encouragement.

"What was your mission?" Steven asked.

Josiah slowly opened his eyes and paused for a long time before he spoke.

"The year was 1886 and my mission was to protect James,

a sharecropper, in Georgia. The years of racial oppression and discrimination shown to him as a young black man made his anger grow. He had a son on the way and he needed to ensure his child would be protected. A few months before I was sent, James was courted by a childhood friend to join a secret fraternal order which protected its members regardless of race and ensured financial security due to the network of individuals involved. My mission was to lead James away from this group in which many of its members were unaware of where it started and why. Fascinated by what membership could bring enticed many to join without asking questions. The order brought food to his wife, Delia, and used their resources to support his family. When hooded men in all white came to his house one night, five of the members of the order, white men, defended his home and forbade them from coming to the house again. They showed James unity, brotherhood, and the power of the fraternal order.

When I became a part of his life, I showed him that he did not need those things from them. They would want something too important to trade in return. Furthermore, I showed him that he had everything he needed all along. I told him that in his blood was greatness. He had the blood of kings. People looked up to him and the words that would be spoken of him, and the life he chose would inspire others and prepare the way for great change. I told him to spend time with his children. Cultivate in them the value of hard work.

I encouraged him to see his calling and continue to lead a life focused on family. I told him to continue to focus on a life where less is more. James and I got into many heated arguments. We fought. Eventually, he decided not to join the group though they courted him for many years. I was sent back to Heaven when his desire for their acceptance was no longer there. He was smitten by something else: the word of God.

James went on to have nine children, the eldest of whom was Michael. Michael married a woman named Alberta. Michael went on to be a preacher, changed his name to Martin and his wife bore a son named after his father—named after the new man he had become. His son led a great movement that changed history, and changed how much of humanity viewed each other." Josiah sat up and reflected on all that he said and smiled.

Steven was in awe of God's plan. Josiah was not given the complete picture when he accepted the mission; he just did what God said. One fateful interaction between one of God's missionaries and His child changed the course of history. Soon Steven would be one of those missionaries and he was no longer scared.

God's voice whispered, "My child, it is time…" Steven's eyelids grew heavy and closed.

***

When he awoke he saw clear blue sky. Suddenly, a large animal stood over him and chewed grass.

"MOOOO," the cow uttered as grass fell from its lips. Steven jumped up and found himself in a large field next to a highway. Cars sped by as Steven looked around, trying to get his bearings. The surroundings were unfamiliar. Steven dusted off his white robe and began walking up the busy highway.

He had no idea what the date was or of anything else for that matter. He had died in the 1930's, and nothing looked the same. There were all types of cars, with all types of odd music blasting. After walking a few miles, he entered a motel to ask the gentleman at the front desk a few questions.

"Hi, sorry to disturb you, could you please tell me where I am?" Steven asked.

The man eyed him strangely. He'd never seen a man, out in public, walking in a long white robe with sandals before.

"You're in Spotsylvania County… Virginia… U-S-A."

Steven was about to walk away, when he remembered what he really wanted to ask.

"Oh! What is the year?"

The man looked slightly agitated.

"It's uh—2016..."

Steven smiled and thanked him. The man watched Steven closely as he left.

"These damn kids need to stop sniffing that paint." The old man mumbled, shook his head, and continued watching TV.

Outside, the sky had begun to fill with clouds. He looked down and three crisp $100 bills were just lying there. Steven looked to see if anyone had dropped them, but there was no one in sight. The clouds opened and sunlight touched his face. He picked it up and whispered, "Thank you, Jesus." He turned back into the motel and asked for a room.

***

Steven knelt by the bed, his hands clasped around each other in prayer. "Jesus, the world is so different from how I remembered it," Steven said. "How will I make it through?"

He prayed for hours, as though Jesus were right there and was given direction regarding his next step.

Steven walked back to the front desk to ask another question. Bothered, the old man stopped reading his paper.

"Hello, again…"

The old man had no response.

"I'm trying to find a friend of mine, but I'm not sure where to start."

The old man pointed to a dusty desktop computer in the lobby. "We have free WiFi… Have at it." The old man continued reading his paper as Steven continued to stand there.

"I'm sorry, WiFi…?"

"Yes… The Internet."

Steven was out of touch and realized figuring out even basic things was going to be challenging. Not wanting to be any more of a nuisance, Steven began to walk away and prayed he'd find someone else.

The old man felt bad. Maybe the boy developed brain damage from sniffing all that paint. He decided to be a bit nicer.

"Hey, buddy… who are you trying to find? I'm Robert by the way."

***

A quick Google search turned up several results for Sarah Michel. She had a few blog posts, a few lengthy articles written about her, and a strong social media presence.

"Is this the gal you're trying to find?" Robert asked.

"Yes, yes, it is!" Steven recognized her face from his conversation with God.

"She's pretty… And you said that's *your* friend?" Robert wanted to do a little investigating of his own, as it seemed very strange that Steven knew nothing about his so called "friend."

"Well, we've never met. But, I want to get to know her. In all honesty, God is leading me to her."

Robert smiled. He was a bit of a romantic himself, and the young man seemed harmless after all. To him, Steven just sounded like a man in love—like he was about forty years ago when he saw his wife for the first time.

"Well, you have to call her. Don't text or email… Call. Chat with her and see where things go from there. She has a contact number here."

Steven wrote down her number and work address. Robert would have paid top dollar to be a fly on the wall when Steven and Sarah met. He knew Steven had no chance of a romantic connection with a woman like her but offered words of encouragement anyway.

"Put your best foot forward, son. If a man landed on the moon, anything's possible."

Steven, thanked Robert, went back to his room, and called Sarah.

*"And give no opportunity to the devil." Ephesians 4:27*

# Chapter Seven

## A Lead

It was around 11:30 PM when Sarah's home business phone rang. That's usually the number people called as a last resort.

"Hello?" She answered.

The call was breaking up and Sarah was not patient enough to wait. Frustrated, she hung up the phone. Thinking it might have been her mother, she unplugged the line.

She turned back over to face the random guy who was naked in her bed. She had brought him back after happy hour and was perplexed that he was still there. She was disgusted by him, he snored, and she heard him fart a few times while he slept. She smacked him on the back of the head to wake him, then quickly repositioned herself.

"Ow..." He uttered as he opened his eyes.

He saw Sarah, fully awake sitting upright in the bed watching CNN. He reached his arm around her waist and rested his head on her lap.

"Hey baby... You ready for round two?"

Sarah rolled her eyes.

"I think it is about time for you to go…"

He sat up with a concerned look on his face.

"Why? We could cuddle…"

Sarah got out of bed and began dressing.

"I don't think that's such a good idea, I have a big day tomorrow, and I just want to get some rest…" Sarah said.

She began picking his clothes off of the floor and throwing them toward him as he instinctively caught each pass. It was awkwardly quiet as he was dressing and she was reorganizing the room.

"Do you want me to call you tomorrow? I felt like we really connected tonight." the guy said, bravely breaking the silence.

Sarah rolled her eyes once again and faced him. She wished he would just stop talking.

"Honestly—what's your name again?" Sarah said as though she was really trying to remember on her own.

"Matthew…" he replied, anxiously awaiting her response.

"Yeah, yeah, Matthew. You're cute and sweet, but it was just sex… That was all. No big deal."

Sarah signaled with her hands toward the space between the both of them.

"This is not going anywhere… Sorry." Sarah said nonchalantly as she shrugged her shoulders.

Matthew chuckled, lifted his eyebrows and lowered his head.

"You can't just use people and then discard them like trash, you know?" Matthew explained.

Sarah looked at him through the reflection in the mirror.

"You know where the exit is. You can see yourself out." She replied as she continued examining her face.

Matthew realized talking to her further would be pointless. He walked out without a word and slammed the door.

***

The next morning, Sarah walked down to the lobby. Her car was waiting for her—just as it should be. The concierge, Anthony, tipped his hat to her but said nothing. She looked at him. He had no smile and looked right through her as he opened the door. It amused her that she had the power to change people's positive attitudes.

When she arrived in the office, she noticed David in the conference room meeting with a few people. David was standing with his sleeves rolled up drawing a graph on the whiteboard. Everyone looked interested in what he was saying. She hurried by, then turned back to peek her head around the corner to get a better look at who was there.

There were about six black people in finely tailored suits. His Intern, Jamal, was taking notes. She had not seen these people before but could tell they were important. Just then, Sarah felt a tap on her shoulder. Startled, she turned around.

"Sorry, Ms. Michel…" Shiloh said.

"You scared the shit out of me, Sally! What is it?"

"Here is your latte and Dr. Bailey has called you four times. I asked him if he would like to leave a message, but he insisted that you call him back."

Sarah sat down at her desk and began checking her email. She sent out feelers to all of her contacts, but all of them said the same thing. No one had a lead. It had been a month and a half since the meeting and she had seen nothing worth presenting to the Board.

Sarah was still highly curious about the morning meeting David was conducting. From her office, she saw David and the group exit the conference room. They were all jovial. The meeting seemed to go well.

David high-fived Jamal as the group turned toward the elevators. David followed them to the lobby and Jamal headed back toward his desk.

Sarah slyly waited a few moments then stepped out of her office and walked down the hall toward David's area. She saw

Jamal in his cubicle.

"Hey… Jay!" Sarah said smiling bigger than ever before.

Jamal spun around in his seat and looked at her.

"My name is Jamal." He replied.

Still smiling, Sarah replied, "Oh, of course, I know, but isn't that what David calls you?"

Jamal continued to stare at her.

"Yeah, that's what *David* calls me, but I know how you are with names, so I wanted to make sure you knew what mine was and how *you* should address me. Speaking of David, he wasn't in his office…?" Jamal asked hoping that she'd understand that he didn't want to be bothered.

Sarah's smile faded a bit.

"Well… Actually Jamal, I came to see you. I wanted to see how you liked the place—and to see if you were settled."

Jamal had been interning in the office since last summer and for most of the fall. She had never uttered one word to him in the hallways, in the break room, in the elevator and now she was concerned about how he liked the place? Jamal was not selected to be a corporate intern for one of the biggest corporations on the eastern sea-board because he was stupid. Understanding where this was going, his response was very direct.

"David gave me strict instructions to direct inquiries about the meeting this morning to him. Therefore, I would suggest you leave a message with his assistant. Or would you prefer I tell him you stopped by and to give you a call?"

Sarah's smile was completely gone at this point. She got his drift. Jamal was not like Shiloh. He had a backbone.

"No thank you, Jamal. It was nice chatting with you." Sarah said, and then quickly walked down the hall.

She looked back and Jamal was standing there, arms folded staring at her. She began to walk faster. When she walked into her office she called for her assistant.

"Sally!"

"Yes…" She replied.

"How well do you know Jamal?" Sarah asked.

"Ah, we have gone to lunch a few times, he is a really nice guy... Why?" Shiloh replied.

"Do you discuss work much?" Sarah asked.

Unsure of where this was going, Shiloh replied, "No... Not really."

"Well, I want you to go to lunch with him and find out what David has been working on lately." Sarah said boldly.

"Ms. Michel, I feel a bit uncomfortable doing that. I mean, Jamal is my friend and I don't want to put him in a weird situation..." Shiloh replied.

This was the only time she had spoken up for herself since she was hired. Sarah stopped what she was doing and decided to use this opportunity to teach a lesson.

"Sally, do you have desires of being anything other than an assistant? If so, this is how the world works. If you want to get ahead, you have to have an edge. You have to know more than your competition." Sarah explained.

Sarah reached into her wallet and handed Shiloh $100.

"Go someplace nice. Have a long lunch. Come back with some information I could use."

Shiloh hesitantly grabbed the money, thanked Sarah and closed her office door.

Sarah went back to checking her email. She saw one from Dr. Bailey.

### RE: PLEASE READ! A LEAD...

*Dear Sarah,*

*Sadly, I had to resort to communicating with you through email because you have returned none of my calls since our last session. I'm sorry.*

*Nonetheless, I know that you are a woman of business and if I am not talking business, my "talking" is not worth your time. Therefore, I have an opportunity for you.*

*My fraternity is having its annual gala in Los Angeles. I have two tickets and would like you to attend. So many well-connected and disgustingly wealthy people attend this event... Someone must have what you need. Please respond.*

*Love,*
*Andrew*

*P.S: I was thinking this could be like a mini get away for us. We could both use one...*

Sarah picked up the phone and dialed.
"Hello? Andrew Bailey speaking."
Sarah smiled as she spun the phone cord around her finger.
"Hi, Andrew... You do know the way to my heart..."

*"Beware of false prophets, who come to you in sheep's clothing but inwardly are ravenous wolves." Matthew 7:15*

# Chapter Eight

## Prey

When Max returned home from school, his room was complete chaos. There were plates piled up with caked up food and empty water bottles everywhere. Jade had been hibernating in his room for a week, eating non-stop, building his energy up again.

"I really like this internet thing..." Jade said as he continued to surf.

"I guess I am going to have to tell Consuela to clean up in here..." Max said as he looked at the floor unsure of where to step.

Max was sixteen years old, very smart, but lonely and misguided. He was abnormally skinny for his height, had acne and braces. He was excluded so much by his peers that he developed his identity around being disliked.

He wore black nail polish, dyed his hair jet black and wore powder on his face to look ghostly. He had become acquainted with the dark arts after meeting a drug dealer at a Rave party who had practiced it. The drug dealer's knowledge and practice of the dark arts was very shallow. He really only did it to look "cool" and attract wild women. But after Max was introduced, he became intrigued and devoted most of his time to studying and learning its concepts. He bought every book, memorized chants, and knew the Satanic bible from cover to cover.

Max's parents were "present" but not really there. His mother was a part of every society club and attended every social function. His father was always busy at work. Max would go weeks without seeing his father, and when he did, his conversations were brief and to the point.

His younger sister, Jessica, was quiet and kept to herself. She tried to spend time with her brother, but he easily became mean and verbally abusive towards her. Max could have had a dead body in his room and his parents would have never known. There was a sign on his door that said, "KEEP OUT" and his parents were great at following directions.

"Are you going to show me how to do some cool tricks now?" Max asked.

"I want a woman." Jade replied as he stared at nude images of women on the internet. Max rolled his eyes.

"Dude… Seriously! Like the whole reason I brought you here was to learn some sick shit!" Max replied unable to hide his frustration.

Jade teleported and stood right behind him.

"Is this what you want to learn?"

Max's eyes opened wide.

"YES! YES! I want to know that stuff!"

Jade assured him that he would learn in due time.

"I am the teacher and you are the student. I will show you all that you need to know, you just have to trust me." Jade said.

Max was mesmerized by him. Jade approached him with a sudden renewed interest. He sniffed Max's body.

"Have you ever experienced a woman?" Jade asked.

"Of course…!" Max replied slightly embarrassed.

Jade smirked. He knew he was lying.

"You have never even kissed a woman before, have you?"

Max lowered his head, trying to hide his rapidly reddening cheeks.

"It is okay, boy. Take me to where there are women." Jade said reassuringly.

***

Max and Jade stood outside the doors of the club. Jade had been attracted to the building's flashing lights and pounding music, and had ordered Max to stop his mother's car.

"Dude… We are so not getting in! This is one of the hottest clubs in Los Angeles." Max said.

"No. This is where we are going." Jade leered at the girls who entered – his eyes full of hunger and wanting. They walked to the front of the line and were immediately stopped by the bouncer.

"See…" Max mumbled convinced there was no way they'd be granted admission.

Jade read the bouncer's mind, then asked him to lean closer. Jade whispered something in his ear and he let both of them through without a second thought.

"What did you say to him?" Max asked.

Jade smiled, "Don't worry about it."

The inside of the club was even more brightly illuminated than the outside. Lights strobed from every direction. The music thumped through their chests. Jade could feel the lust in the air as he gazed at the women gyrating upon the dance floor. He would like this place.

Max watched Jade closely as they walked through the crowd. A woman stepped out of the crowd and grabbed Jade's hand. He stopped and they looked at each other for about three minutes. He leaned in and kissed her. Max was shocked. Jade had done nothing. As they kissed, another woman came from behind, seductively turned Jade's face towards her and greeted him with an equally intense kiss. Jade whispered into the first woman's ear. She nodded and put her hands around Max's neck. She shoved her tongue down his throat. Max backed away, surprised. He caught his breath and went back for seconds. Jade laughed and put his arm around Max's shoulder.

"Just live in the moment. Let whatever happens… happen… Go with the flow." Jade advised.

Max licked his lips as Jade waved the bartender over. The group partied the rest of the night.

***

"This has been the best night of my life!" Max screamed as Jade drove his mother's car through the night. "I feel like I am finally living, man! The only person I kicked it with like this was a drug dealer who just used me for my money. I knew it and didn't care! But you're actually going to show me shit, and be here for me… You're my best friend, dude…"

Jade looked in the rear view mirror at Max as he passed out from the drinks. Jade knew Max did not really want power, he wanted friendship. Max trusted Jade. He considered Jade a friend—his best friend. That's where Jade wanted him.

***

The next morning Max was still passed out on his bedroom floor. Jade came out of the shower and wrapped a towel around his waist, when he noticed the door ajar. Jade remained still and watched the door. A young girl walked in, tip toeing as though she were looking for something.

"Here kitty, kitty…" Jessica said.

Jade continued to watch her. She had not noticed him. She had long brown hair, glasses, and olive colored skin. She was beautiful.

"Hello…" Jade said.

Jessica popped up startled. Her eyes wide open with fear.

"Who are you?" She asked.

Jade smiled.

"My name is Jade. I am a friend of your brother's. He has told me a lot about you."

Jessica looked at the floor and saw her brother lying there not moving.

"What did you do to my brother?" Her eyes began watering.

"Nothing. He's hungover." Jade replied.

Jessica began to run for the door, but Jade made it shut. She jiggled the knob, but it would not open. She was about to scream when Jade interjected.

"Don't scream, Jessica—I'm not going to hurt you. Think about it: if I were going to hurt you, I would have done it long ago. I just want to talk to you. Come here."

She looked at him. He still had droplets of water dripping down his chiseled chest and abs. She was obviously afraid but more curious. She inched closer and closer until she was standing right in front of him. She looked into his eyes. They were green, but his pupils were the largest she had ever seen. They were black, but they were so gorgeous. They stared at each other in silence. Jade took her hands gently and interlocked their fingers.

"How old are you, Jessica?" He whispered.

"I'm thirteen…" She replied innocently.

Jade removed her curly hair from her face. He caressed the back of her arms and she began to feel comfortable with him. The fear faded.

"You are a woman now… Are you not?" Jade knew that she had gotten her first period about two weeks ago.

Jessica blushed with embarrassment and tried to pull away. Jade tightened his grip on the back of her arm, pulling her closer.

"Don't be shy around me, Jessica. I know what you feel." He removed her glasses and rested them on the bed.

"You're beautiful, and you're brave. I can tell by your reaction to me. You are a woman now, and you have to start using your mind and your body to get what you want. Even the strongest men will bend to you Jessica." Jade said seductively.

She nodded. He placed one hand on her head, and placed the other on her inner thigh and then moved his hand further up her skirt. Jessica's eyes closed and her body melted in his arms. She shivered as he felt her.

"May I kiss you Jessica...?" Jade asked anticipating her answer.

Unable to speak, she nodded. He pressed his lips against hers and slowly placed his tongue on top hers. She wrapped her arms around his neck and began to kiss him passionately. Max began moving on the floor.

"Where am I?" he said disoriented.

Jade stopped her and pushed her away gently and quickly sat on the bed. Jade placed one finger over his lips and smiled at Jessica. That was their secret, and a moment Jessica would never forget. Max struggled to stand when he saw Jade sitting on the bed and Jessica pressed against the wall breathing heavily. Her eyes were completely focused on Jade.

"Jessica, get the HELL OUT!" Max yelled.

Jessica ignored her brother, until Jade smiled and gestured for her to leave. Before she left, Jade whispered, "Remember what I told you." Jessica blushed and hurried down the hall.

"Are you feeling better?" Jade asked.

"Yeah, a little bit..." Max said as he rubbed his temples.

"Good." Jade rose, and dragged Max to his feet. "You have to take me to Hollywood."

Max was surprised this was what he had to do after just waking up, but he was willing to do anything Jade asked at this point. Jade was the teacher and Max was ready and willing to learn.

As they were backing out of the driveway, Jade looked up, and there was Jessica standing on the balcony. She blew him a kiss. She was smitten by him. She knew in her heart that would be the last time she would see him, but she would dream of him for years to come.

***

Max stopped the car in front of a large gated estate.

"This is it…" Jade said.

Max pulled into a nearby alley at Jade's direction. Jade reached into his bag.

"I got you something…" he said.

Jade knew that Max was impressionable. He would move wherever the wind blew him. More than anything, he wanted a friend—someone to confide in. If he had not found the dark arts first, it could have very well been Christianity or anything that showed him some form of acceptance. This made him dangerous. He could be easily coaxed into anything—and at this point, he knew too much. Jade withdrew a small object, wrapped in black cloth. Max unwrapped the package, handling his gift with care; inside the bundle was a gun. Max looked up at Jade, and his eyes began to water.

"Max, you said you wanted to be like me and know what I know… Well, this is the first step."

Max's hand shook violently as he put the gun to his head.

"I will become powerful, right?" Max asked needing reassurance.

Jade knew that once Max went to Hell, he did not have the hate needed to become demonic. He would never pass the test. He had too much sadness. If Max went to Hell, he would be just another tormented soul for eternity. Jade could not care less. Max was going to be first of many reasons Jade had to remain on earth for as long as possible. Jade looked at him and said, "Trust me…"

One shot broke the driver's side window. Max's head dropped on the steering wheel. Without a second thought, Jade grabbed his bag and ran out of the alley. He continued up the street to the house. The sign above the gate read, "LINDEN". Jade pressed the buzzer.

"Who is it?" a voice asked.

"It is Jade, here to see Samuel Linden."

The gate opened as a voice said, "We have been expecting you."

*"Because the sentence against an evil deed is not executed speedily, the heart of the children of man is fully set to do evil." Ecclesiastes 8:11*

# Chapter Nine

## Follow the Leader

The home of Samuel Linden was hideously opulent. He had expensive white and brown marble floors, a spiral staircase, enormous Persian rugs, beautiful vases, and notable paintings neatly hung throughout his Mansion. The home was fit for a king.

A maid escorted Jade to the living room where he sat and waited. There was a perfect view to the outside where the pool looked like it blended with the horizon. There were about ten people laughing outside and sunbathing.

"Welcome to my home, Jade." Samuel said as he walked into the living room with open arms.

Jade stood up and smiled.

"Mr. Linden, how are you?"

"Please call me Sam. Our *friend* said you would be handsome, but I was not expecting perfection!" Sam joked. "Follow me, we have much to discuss!"

Sam was a man small in stature—no taller than 5'5. He

was in great shape with a lean muscular physique. As they headed upstairs, Jade made a note of the walls lined with photos of Sam with movie stars, singers, and politicians.

"These look like some very important people," Jade said.

"And they're all playing for a winning team," Sam replied, smiling deviously.

Sam's office was festooned with numerous awards, plaques and medals. Sam took a seat in a gigantic leather chair—clearly too large for his small frame, as Jade continued to look at the walls.

"Humanitarian of the year?" Jade asked as he looked back at Sam jokingly.

"I know, right!? It's all about who you know, right?"

Jade finally sat down, still scanning the room.

"You have done extremely well for yourself." Jade complimented. Sam poured himself a glass of Cognac.

"Yeah… Well, Satan doesn't keep you on earth for centuries unless you're doing something right."

Jade wanted to be like him. Earth was heavenly compared to hell. Jade cringed at the thought of having to return. He wanted to enjoy the money and the women all over again. If it took lying, cheating, and killing to keep this lifestyle, he would do it, and he was certain many humans would do it too if it meant they could live like this.

Sam stood abruptly, turning to gaze out the window.

"I get more souls in a day, than most demons could get in 10 years." He said confidently. Jade was even more attentive than before.

"You see… I don't do all the work myself. I never have. And demons aren't the ones working for me either; they of course are working for themselves. I have humans working for me." Sam explained.

Sam began to pace around the room as though he were giving a presentation.

"You're referring to humans who practice the dark arts?" Jade said as though he were already privy to this information.

Sam smiled and shook his head.

"No, the best people I have working for me don't even know what they're doing. They're oblivious to the bigger picture. Sam raised his pinky finger. There was a gold ring, gleaming just beneath the knuckle. "Do you know what this is?"

Jade scrutinized it—the letters GMA were engraved on its side.

"This was the ring I would give to people who became a part of my group when it began in 1800. Now, the group has grown to over two million people strong—worldwide. One must work for this ring. Only the richest, most influential, and successful people are a part of this group. And guess what Jade? Everyone wants in. People will do anything, and I mean anything for membership. The whole group is built on secrecy and exclusivity. There are many groups similar to mine. But it's all the same. Hell, I trained the leaders who started many of those organizations. The people who are already members have done things—small and insignificant at first, but progressively more heinous. Every bit of it furthered Satan's agenda. Deep down they know that, and yet… They were willing—simply because in the end they move up the ladder. We have made small time entrepreneurs into corporate giants; we have made average men into Presidents. There is a quid pro quo to becoming a part of this organization, you must give, and the only thing of value is your soul. Eventually, these are the people who become the leaders and the decision makers. They advance our agenda. Then people follow. Why become their leader? People always need someone to follow."

Jade was impressed by Sam's vision, and the simple formula he applied to acquiring the human soul worked wonders. Jade began to confide in Sam.

"I have been here for a week, and I have gotten only one soul. I have to do better…" Jade said a bit disappointed.

Sam offered Jade a cigar and lit one himself.

"You will do better. We are living in times where the stage is set for us. Sometimes our best move is waiting. I came from an age where any talk of Satan was intolerable; it was a lot harder to lead them away because so many people feared God. Now there are so many things humans are into and tolerate. It has become so much easier to plant the seed. You and I both know that one need not worship Satan to go to Hell. Humans truly are curious creatures. How can so many people believe in Heaven and not believe there is a Hell? Humans love to pick and choose the parts of God's law that is easiest to follow. They even go as far as convincing themselves and others they are actually following Christ, fully aware they are not doing all that is required of them. That is the denial you can really build on." Sam said.

Sam went on to explain that he had over ten bedrooms in his house and Jade could stay with him until he found his own niche with acquiring souls.

Sam handed Jade the ring the two were discussing.

"Here, now you are a high ranking Gratis Meson; see for yourself where membership takes you."

*"And no wonder, for even Satan disguises himself as an angel of light."* 2 *Corinthians 11:14*

# Chapter Ten

## The Gala

Sarah felt on top of the world. She was all smiles as she put on her make-up and lipstick. Shiloh was unable to get the information she wanted, but surprisingly, Sarah was not upset by her lack of effort. Truthfully, she was just happy that she was going to see Dr. Andrew Bailey again. The idea of him thinking of her for this important event and thinking of her career meant more to Sarah than any romantic gesture. He sent Sarah both her plane ticket and gala ticket. Enclosed was a note:

*Dear Sarah,*

*I am so happy you agreed to attend this event. I will be waiting for you at LAX. I will take care of everything; don't worry about a thing.*

*Love,*
*Andrew*

Sarah read the letter one more time before she packed it away in her carryon luggage.

When Sarah arrived at the airport, Andrew was waiting there dressed casually and wearing sunglasses. She smiled as she walked towards him. She greeted him with a warm kiss on the cheek then whispered in his ear.

"You know exactly how to get back on my good side." She said jokingly.

Andrew smirked as he followed her into the town car. They could not keep their hands off each other. When they arrived at the hotel, they maintained their composure until they reached the room where they resumed passionately kissing.

"Wait, I want to show you something," Andrew said.

Sarah smiled, "What is it?"

"You have to close your eyes," He said as he placed his hands over her eyes to ensure they were closed.

He guided her toward the closet and opened the doors. He gently removed his hands, Sarah opened her eyes and her mouth dropped. It was a long black satin gown that was tailored beautifully and was perfect for her frame.

"I want you to wear this dress to the Gala this evening. You will be stunning." Andrew said.

Speechless, Sarah began to kiss him. She laid him on the bed and they made love.

***

Sarah reached over to place her hands on Andrew's chest, but could only feel the warmth of the sheets. His absence woke her. Sarah sat up and caught Andrew putting on his clothes.

"Hey… Where are you going?" Sarah said as she reached for his hand. Andrew looked back at her and smiled.

"The Gala starts soon; I have to get ready." He replied as he continued dressing.

Sarah looked around and noticed none of his things were in

the room.

"So… You're not getting ready here?" Sarah asked.

"This is your room baby; I have my own." Andrew replied.

Confused, Sarah got up and approached him.

"I thought this was going to be our time…" Sarah said flirtatiously.

Andrew cupped her face in his hands.

"It will be… After the Gala."

He kissed her forehead and started for the door.

"There will be a car waiting for you in an hour; I will see you there. Don't be late." he said.

Andrew closed the door behind him. Sarah plopped in the bed and spoke to herself.

"I guess this is better than nothing, right?"

***

Sarah arrived at the hotel right on time. She looked beautiful in the dress Andrew had gotten her. The only person she knew was Andrew, and she wanted to wait for him to escort her inside.

Just then a limo pulled up and the driver opened the door. Andrew stepped out and looked around. He looked amazing. Sarah thought he must have been looking for her. She was about to walk towards him, when he turned back to the car and reached in to help a woman out of the limo. It was his wife.

Sarah quickly turned around; her heart felt like it was going to jump out of her chest. If she could hide under a rock, she would. She started to head for the entrance, when she heard Andrew's voice.

"Sarah? Wait a second…"

Inside, Sarah was furious and could not believe he had the audacity to even acknowledge her with his wife present. Andrew approached with his wife firmly affixed to his arm.

"Good evening Sarah. You look stunning. You do remember my wife Rachael?"

Sarah and Rachael met briefly about six years ago during a Christmas party Andrew held at his home.

"Oh... Yes, I remember your wife..." Sarah said as she extended her hand to greet her.

Rachael smiled and embraced her.

"How have you been Sarah?" Rachael asked as she rubbed her back. "I hope things have gotten better for you."

When Rachael pulled away, there was an uncomfortable silence, and the three stood there awkwardly for a few moments.

"Well honey, I'm going to say hello to Mrs. Fienberg... It was so nice seeing you again Sarah." Rachael said, trying her hardest to politely mask her discomfort.

Sarah stared at Rachael as she walked away. Rachael made her sick. She was the type of woman who was brilliant enough to be successful on her own, but was content to be a trophy wife and just stay home to raise kids.

"When were you going to tell me your wife was going to be here?" Sarah whispered.

"I didn't know she was coming! She told me she probably wouldn't come this year because she was going to see her sister. She called me a day before and said she changed her mind and would come. She's leaving tomorrow, we have time..." Andrew said.

"Andrew, this is strictly a business trip now. Spend time with your wife!" Sarah said.

A man approached them. He was short and eccentric looking.

"Andrew, so glad you could make it."

"How could I miss a Samuel Linden event?" Andrew replied. The two of them embraced briefly and laughed.

"Who is this beauty you have on your arm?" Samuel asked.

"Pardon, this is Sarah Michel. A good friend of mine..." Andrew said.

Samuel kissed her hand and Sarah smiled.

"Andrew, you wouldn't mind if I introduced Ms. Michel to

a few people, would you?"

Before Andrew could reply, Sarah interjected.

"Oh, of course he doesn't mind. I think his wife will be looking for him soon, and I will be left all alone."

Samuel extended his arm; Sarah placed her arm inside and confidently began to walk with him. Samuel introduced her to almost everyone, and Sarah loved it. These were some of the wealthiest and most well-connected people in the country. She smiled, she laughed, she gathered business cards; and most importantly, she could tell that Andrew was jealous. At times Sarah would look up and catch Andrew staring from across the room.

Sarah stepped onto the balcony for a moment to herself. It was a warm night, but the light breeze made her chilly and she shivered. As her eyes scanned the night sky, she caught a glimpse of a shadowy figure standing in the corner of the balcony. She squinted, but could only see the frame.

"You look cold…" a voice said.

"I am slightly… I cannot see you…" Sarah replied.

He began to walk slowly into the light. The more the light revealed his physique, the more Sarah liked him.

He was tall, had beautiful green eyes, dark hair, smooth skin, and the perfect smile. He was gorgeous. Sarah tried to catch her breath and keep her cool as he walked towards her.

Jade removed his jacket and placed it over her shoulders. They both leaned on the railing and looked at the stars. They were silent, but it was a comfortable silence. They were content in each other's presence.

Sarah looked at him and he looked at her. They both smiled.

"Who are you?" Sarah asked

"My name is Jade. I'm not as important as these people."

He chuckled, pulled out a cigarette and offered her one. Sarah eyed him and gently removed a cigarette from the pack. She laughed to herself because she knew there was no possible way that he was unimportant. They stood closer to each other. Their interaction was so natural that one could easily assume they had known each other for years. Sarah looked back at the crowded room. Andrew was staring at her. Sarah wanted to keep the show going.

"Do you want to get out of here?" Sarah asked spontaneously.

Jade, with an equal amount of spontaneity, grabbed her hand and headed for the front entrance.

***

Jade and Sarah stared at the ceiling as they laid in her hotel bed. The two of them had shared two bottles of red wine. They had talked for close to three hours about work and their philosophies on life. Jade mostly listened to Sarah and was intrigued by her. He liked the way her mouth moved, and the way she smiled.

"What do you believe in?" Jade asked.

"What?" Sarah replied as she laughed. The question caught her off guard. "I guess, I believe in the tooth fairy and Santa Claus..." Sarah joked.

"I'm serious. Do you believe in God?" Jade asked as he leaned over her.

"God hasn't done too much for me..." Sarah stopped laughing and became reflective. "I don't believe in much of anything." She said.

Jade smiled and laid back down. Sarah grabbed his hand and looked at his ring.

"So what is this?"

Jade sat back up again and leaned in closer to Sarah. He removed the ring and turned it in his fingers.

"This ring represents attaining the highest level of membership in the Order." Jade replied.

Sarah was interested. Andrew had a similar ring, but it was not as nice as Jade's.

"So what did you have to do to get that ring?" Sarah said, using the conversation as an opportunity to be more flirtatious.

"This ring represents the level of knowledge and awareness I have…" Jade replied.

"Your knowledge and awareness of what?" Sarah prodded.

Jade looked at her and smiled.

"My knowledge of everything…"

She was curious, and curiosity was all he needed.

"Sarah, this ring represents a world you have yet to experience. The person wearing this ring could open more doors for you and can show you more than you can ever imagine. We are the Grand Master Architects. Should you ever meet someone wearing this ring, you should listen to whatever it is he has to say. If you do not believe in anything, Sarah, believe in us."

Sarah's heart was pounding as she looked in his eyes. She had always wanted those connections—these friends in high places. She did not know much about Jade's background, but to her it did not matter. She knew he had connections, and he had clout.

Jade knew that the seed had been planted with Sarah. He could tell that she liked him for all of the wrong reasons. Their entire interaction was based on physical attraction and everything that the eyes could easily gather. He learned more about her than she knew about him. Jade believed that she may have even thought he was a good guy.

Jade leaned in to kiss her. Their lips almost touched when she pulled away. Jade gently grabbed the back of her neck, and Sarah put up a playful resistance. Jade could feel that Sarah was not completely there with him. At this point, Jade had been acquiring souls easier than he had expected. After Max, he met people who all but handed their souls to him. They were easily influenced and nudging them in the direction he wanted them to go was all it took. There was something about her that was telling him she could be redeemed, and he wanted her. Jade knew it would take some work to get her to pledge her allegiance, but he was willing to put in the work. She would be a fun challenge. She reminded him of someone he knew but could not remember. Jade was intrigued by her complexity. Her soul became his project.

Jade lifted Sarah up and held her body close to his. He looked into her eyes and leaned in to kiss her. He paused before he touched her lips, and she smiled. They kissed as Jade unzipped and slowly removed her dress before he threw it to the floor. Sarah reached for the switch and turned out the light.

*"So then, as we have opportunity, let us do good to everyone, and especially to those who are of the household of faith." Galatians 6:10*

# Chapter Eleven

## The World

Steven got on a bus for Washington, D.C. He took a vacant seat close to the back next to a kid. The boy could not have been older than twelve, but his clothes were clearly three sizes too big. Steven looked curiously at the boy who was aggressively bobbing his head to music. Though the kid had headphones on, the music was loud enough for Steven to hear.

Steven tapped the boy on the shoulder and asked, "What are you listening to?"

The boy removed his headphones and looked very annoyed.

"What...?" he replied.

"I was just wondering what you were listening to." Steven said politely.

"Rap music." The boy said.

The boy placed his headphones on and continued to bob his head. Steven tapped him on the shoulder again.

"May, I listen?"

The boy looked at him like he was crazy and begrudgingly extended one of the earpieces so he could hear.

Steven listened to the music and was so disturbed he immediately handed the earpiece back to him. The boy looked confused.

"What, you don't like it?"

Steven shook his head.

"No, not at all..."

The boy laughed.

"You're a goody-goody ain't you?"

Steven looked at the boy, and though he was very young, Steven could tell that he was wise beyond his years.

"Why do you like that music?" Steven asked.

"Cause it's cool..." The boy replied.

"Why is it cool?" Steven asked.

"I don't know—because it talks about everything I want in life: money, girls, cars, power, doing what you want... *You* don't want that?"

Steven gave no reaction and the boy immediately started laughing.

"You're trippin'... For real! You makin' me think you a little funny..."

Steven cracked a smile. There was something about the boy Steven liked. Steven could tell that he was good, he was just misguided. The two continued to talk.

"Where is your mother?" Steven asked.

"She lives in Northeast, that's who I'm gonna see..."

"Why were you away from her?" Steven asked.

"Unfortunately, I had to spend three months in this boy's home and do whack-ass community service, because I had stolen some stuff from a convenience store."

"What did you steal?" Steven asked.

"A bag of chips and a soda..."

"Why?"

"I was dared to by my boys. I had to." The boy said.

"Why did you have to?" Steven asked.

"Cause they would think I was a bamma if I didn't, that I was scared." The boy replied trying to establish common ground.

"Oh, I see... Cause you had to look cool, right?" Steven said.

"I guess you could say that." The boy said relieved that Steven finally understood something he was saying.

"What did you miss most while you were in the boy's home?"

"You know, you ask a lot of questions." The boy cut his eyes at Steven. "I don't know. I missed my little sister. She was only a month old when I left. She is probably really big now, and I missed my mom and my grandmother." The boy replied.

"I notice you did not say your boys..."

"Nah, I didn't think about them too much while I was there."

"So you missed precious time with your little sister, your mom, and your grandmother for a bag of chips and a soda? Was it worth it?" Steven asked.

The boy paused and reflected.

"I never thought about it like that... But no, it wasn't worth it."

"People never consider the bigger picture in the moment. I bet you never thought that one simple act could remove you from your family. You probably never thought about how your absence affected them. We do not live in isolation. Instead, we are connected to each other. What you do matters. What you say matters. Who you are matters. If you think about things that way, the way you live each day becomes much more significant." Steven said.

For the first time in a long time, the boy did not laugh or shrug his shoulders or give off the nonchalant attitude that so many of his friends admired. For the first time in a long time he listened. Steven could tell that the words he spoke resonated with the child.

"Hey... What's your name, man?" the boy asked.

"My name is Steven, and yours?"

"My name is Carlos."

Steven extended his hand and they shook.

***

As the bus approached the city, an eerie feeling consumed Steven's body. His senses were heightened and everything in his spirit was telling him to be on alert. Carlos nudged Steven and prodded him to look at the monuments. Steven's face moved closer to the glass, and his eyes widened as he saw signs and symbols he knew were not of God, but had become what the boy would call "cool". Steven closed his eyes and began to pray silently. The boy looked at him and as a sign of compassion rested his hand on his shoulder.

"Yeah… If this is your first time in the city, things can be overwhelming. Chill, though… You'll love it!"

When the bus arrived at the terminal, Steven walked off and was waiting next to Carlos in line as the attendant placed bags on the curb. Steven turned around and looked toward the sky. He was taking in everything around him. When his eyes came back to earth, he saw a demon approaching him! The beast was the most frightening sight he had ever seen.

Steven hurriedly back-peddled so far that he tripped over a few bags. The irritated crowd started yelling, "Watch it!"

The boy helped him up and asked, "Are you ok?"

The demon was standing right next to Carlos. The image of the demon faded, to reveal a very attractive guy.

"Is this guy OK?" the demon asked.

Carlos answered for Steven.

"Yeah, yeah, he's good… He just ain't from here."

The demon handed Carlos a flier.

"Yo, this new club is FIRE, son! Tell your boy to loosen up and come out…"

Carlos took the flier, looked at it and smiled.

"Aight…"

Carlos gave the demon a pound and he walked off.

Steven watched the demon carefully as he walked away. Steven remembered he was the only one who could see them for what they really were. He knew that if he were to avoid being detected, he would have to do a better job of keeping his composure.

When Steven stood up, he looked around and noticed dozens of demons walking among humans; none of whom realized what was approaching them on the sidewalk, what was sitting across the table, or what was whispering in their ear.

"Ok, it was cool talking to you…" Carlos said.

Steven, clearly preoccupied, replied, "Yes, yes… God bless you."

As Carlos began to walk off, he turned back to look at Steven. Steven was standing on the sidewalk looking to the sky. Under normal circumstances the boy would have just left and never thought about him again. But something in his heart told him not to leave him.

"Yo! Steve!" Carlos yelled.

Steven looked around and found Carlos further up the block.

"Come on!" Carlos said as he signaled for him to follow.

***

When they arrived at Carlos's mother's apartment, Carlos knocked. After a few moments, his mother opened the door. Without hesitation she happily embraced her son.

"I missed you so much, chico!" She hugged him for so long that at first she did not notice Steven standing there. When she looked up, she was startled.

"Who are you?"

Before Steven could answer, Carlos interjected.

"Ma, he's cool…"

His mother excused herself, ushered her son in the

apartment and closed the door. His mother spoke Spanish and the boy replied in English. They were talking loud enough for Steven to hear.

"Yes Ma, I know, there are a bunch of crazies out here… No, he didn't touch me… He just needs food… Ma, relax!"

After about five minutes the door reopened.

"Well, I guess you're just in time for dinner. My name is Maria." His mother said politely.

***

Steven sat on the couch and watched Carlos play with his little sister. He smiled because it reminded him of the children by the river in Heaven. The baby kept staring at Steven, while giggling and reaching for him.

"Yo, she likes you a lot!" Carlos said.

Steven humbly smiled and continued to watch them play. Though Maria's back was turned, she was very attentive to all that was happening in the living room.

"So, where are you from?" Maria asked.

"Oh… I am from way up north…" Steven replied vaguely.

"Really…? From where—" Maria asked.

Before she could finish her question a loud crack of thunder diverted her attention outside. It was raining heavily.

Steven looked up and whispered, "Thank you, GOD!"

Maria went back to cooking. Maria was young and was naturally beautiful; she had taken on so much responsibility when others had abandoned theirs. She was strong.

Carlos' father died four years ago. Her daughter's father was sent to jail on drug charges, and her mother had a stroke, which left her unable to speak. What little money Maria had saved, she put toward cancer treatments and medications. The doctors told her there was nothing else they could do. Cancer was eating away at her mother's body and the time was looming. With all this weighing on Maria's mind and heart, she still took the time to prepare a good meal for a stranger and share what little she had.

As the three new friends sat around the table, prayed, and ate, the discomfort faded. They laughed and momentarily forgot about their troubles.

When they finished eating, Steven helped clean off the table. Maria glanced at him warmly. Steven caught her, and she quickly looked away. Steven smiled at her and thanked her for dinner as he headed toward the front door.

"It is pouring outside... You can sleep on the couch..." Maria said.

"Oh, it is okay, I wouldn't want to inconvenience you." Steven said.

"Please, stay..." Maria said.

He nodded politely acquiescing.

***

Steven was leaving the bathroom when he noticed Carlos kneeling by the bed in the room where his Grandmother was.

"I love you Abuela" Carlos said.

Steven watched as Carlos' grandmother, weak and in pain, lovingly stroked his hair. Steven watched from afar until Carlos left for his own room. Steven quietly snuck into the Grandmother's room.

Though she could not speak, her eyes were warm, speaking volumes. She could feel his goodness. Steven sat in a chair close to the bed. The old woman signaled for him to bring his ear close to her lips. Steven began speaking to her as though he were replying to questions. Maria walked by the room and swiftly stepped back to see Steven praying with her mother. Steven looked up and extended his hand to Maria. "It is time..."

Maria's eyes immediately began to water and she rushed for her mother's hand.

"Mama! Please don't leave me! Please, I need you!" Maria cried.

She lovingly looked into her daughter's eyes before they slowly closed. Maria and Steven watched as her chest rose, then collapsed. She had taken her final breath.

Maria screamed, "MAMA!"

Carlos rushed into the room. He needed no explanation: he understood what transpired. He embraced his mother as they both cried.

Steven led them in the Lord's Prayer:

>Our Father who art in heaven, hallowed be thy name, thy kingdom come, thy will be done on earth as it is in heaven…"

*"No temptation has overtaken you that is not common to man. God is faithful, and he will not let you be tempted beyond your ability, but with the temptation he will also provide the way of escape, that you may be able to endure it." 1 Corinthians 10:31*

# Chapter Twelve

## The Proposition

When Sarah returned to the office, she was on cloud nine. She returned from her trip with a newfound sense of superiority. She had been introduced to an elite world others had not an inkling of. No longer would she ever feel like an outsider needing to beat down doors and pound the pavement for contacts; she "knew" people now, and not just rich people, but extraordinarily rich people. David popped into her office at the exact moment she hoped he would.

"So, how was LA?" David asked.

"Oh, it was absolutely wonderful; I attended a Gratis event..." Sarah said casually.

"Well, aren't you the 'A' lister..." David replied.

Sarah loved the fact that he knew the importance of the event.

"I knew a few people. Samuel Linden guest listed me. Have you heard of him?"

David looked at her and smiled.

"Ah… Yeah… He might be one of the most influential socialites of our time, but his crowd was never my cup of tea."

Sarah cut her eyes at him. She did not think it was possible, but yet again David managed to piss her off.

"Why, might I ask, would a group of the most successful, influential, and powerful men not be *your* cup of tea, David?" Sarah asked sarcastically.

"Hey, I didn't mean anything by it! It's just that when groups become too exclusive, I start to question what they are really about. Yes, the Gratis Mesons are very 'successful,' but for a group with so much power, they have not done too much for the world, other than continually reinforce how great it is to be ridiculously wealthy." David said as he took a seat.

Sarah folded her arms and leaned back in her chair.

"Sour grapes, David? You sound like someone who wanted to be one but never could." Sarah replied.

David laughed and politely corrected her.

"Well… You are partially right, I have never been a Gratis Meson. I turned them down."

Sarah rolled her eyes thinking either he was lying or life was playing a very cruel joke on her. Of course David would have been offered membership to one of the most exclusive organizations in the world and declined; he was so much above it all. At this point, Sarah had to know why.

"Well, I was offered membership right out of college, but I had already decided to join the Peace Corps. I got a lot of flak from my friends and even my family who claimed my opportunities would be boundless once I joined, but I decided to take my chances. Once I got accepted to Yale, while doing my JD/MBA, the opportunity was presented to me again. But after spending two years in Rwanda, there was no way I could join a group just to say I am a part of something. There were things that became so much more important to me and labels and affiliations were not on my list. What makes me want to be a part of 'something' is what it is they are doing for humanity. I am less concerned about who is a part of the group. Unfortunately, the Gratis Meson's weren't doing enough for me."

She felt that David wasn't telling the truth. No one could really feel that way. She didn't, the world didn't, and anyone who claimed otherwise was either lying or a fool.

"This was a nice chat David, but I must get back to work." Sarah said, cutting the conversation short.

David shrugged his shoulders, briskly got up and left the room.

Sarah rolled her eyes again when the phone rang.

"Hello, is this Sarah Michel?"

"And this is—?"

"This is Leonardo DeAmato, we exchanged cards at the Gratis event…"

Sarah quickly sifted through her cards, and there he was, Leonardo DeAmato, president of Future Intellect, Inc. The company was designing and working on non-lethal weaponry prototypes for the past 10 years. They were not well known, but held a few patents and had the potential to make a great deal of money. They had not done so yet.

"Yes, Mr. DeAmato, I was planning on calling you today." Sarah said.

"Oh great, that must mean we are both thinking about money. Please call me DeAmato. All my friends call me DeAmato. There is no need to be so formal." Sarah chuckled and loosened up a bit.

"If it wouldn't be too much of an inconvenience for you, would you be available to stop by my hotel in the city for a quick presentation by my staff? We have a proposition that might be of interest to you." DeAmato offered.

Sarah's eyes widened. She was surprised at how things were progressing rather easily since the event. She eagerly agreed.

***

When Sarah arrived, she was escorted to the hotel conference room. DeAmato pulled out a chair for her and she took a seat. She noted the smiles of those seated—all except one, a thin man of Indian appearance who looked slightly nervous. Sarah acknowledged their graciousness.

"We are so glad you could come on short notice." DeAmato said as he took a seat at the far end of the conference table.

"Imagine a world where the risk involved in fighting crime is drastically reduced. Imagine a world where a police officer can apprehend an assailant safely 100 percent of the time. Take a moment to think how many more police officers would make it home to their families and live to fight crime another day. This is all possible with Future Intellect, Inc." DeAmato said.
Sarah appeared to be listening intently. She wished he would get to the point—the end—the money. The lights dimmed and one of the team members took over the presentation. On the screen, a picture of what looked like a hand-held scanner used in grocery stores appeared. "This is the Crime Halter. This device uses the latest laser technology that literally freezes a suspect in his or her tracks for approximately 15 minutes. It acts as a high powered "muscle relaxer" which targets the Central Nervous System. The laser completely impairs movement. This allows a police officer to safely approach, frisk, and hand cuff the suspect without fear of death or bodily harm."

Sarah was amazed.

"How is this possible?" she asked.

"We'll show you now…"

The young lady giving the presentation grabbed the device out of her bag, pointed it at her male teammate and paralyzed him. Sarah jumped out of her seat.

"WHAT ARE YOU DOING!?" Sarah screamed.

DeAmato approached Sarah.

"It's okay; it is all a part of the presentation…" DeAmato said, reassuringly. Sarah cautiously returned to her seat and continued to watch. The young lady approached her colleague who was completely still.

"Are you okay?" she asked.

He replied, "Yes, I am."

"As you can see, the suspect will still be able to speak. However, he will not be able to move any other part of his body on his own. Does anything hurt?" She asked him.

"Nope—completely fine." He replied.

The young lady walked toward Sarah and changed the slide.

"This device will make the Taser virtually obsolete. Not only will this device keep the officer safe, it also causes no harm to the suspect. Our studies show that this device will reduce lawsuits due to police brutality by 65 percent. A survey we recently conducted of 100 American chiefs of police, sheriffs, and deputy sheriffs asked if they would use a device like this in their precincts showed that 98% said yes." The young lady finished.

DeAmato leaned closer to Sarah and raised his eyebrows.

"What do you think?"

Sarah was impressed—but wouldn't dare show it.

"So why do you need me?"

"Well, truthfully, your company has stood the test of time; it is a household name and has earned the trust of the American people. Though we are a company that has been building a name for ourselves, there is still much hesitancy with us. We are a fairly new Italian business, and we first need the American market to accept us before the world will. Your monetary strength to fund a few more of our projects would not hurt either." DeAmato said with a smile.

Sarah knew this was a game changer. Of course they

needed the money to manufacture the device, which her company could easily cover, but the revenue would be worth the expense. She could see every police officer in the world using this device— every prison guard, every solider—even every psychiatric worker and kindergarten teacher.

"We'll think about it." Sarah replied, tactfully.

As she stood up, the team formed a line and each approached to shake her hand. They were all smiling and happy about the prospects, except the Indian gentleman. He looked Sarah directly in the eyes and shook her hand unenthusiastically. Sarah's face tightened out of disdain for his demeanor, but she continued to ignore his rudeness. DeAmato walked Sarah outside.

"Exciting, isn't it?" DeAmato said.

"Yes… It certainly is." Sarah replied.

"It is bringing us one step closer to a time we all have been hoping for…" DeAmato said.

"No more senseless killing. A time of peace, right?" Sarah said with a genuine smile.

"Yes... Peace…"

He tried hard to conceal the devilish grin that was growing on his face. Sarah smiled back as the town car approached. She was about to step in when she turned back to DeAmato.

"Do you want to hear something funny?" Sarah asked.

DeAmato cocked his head to the side quizzically.

"A colleague of mine said that the Gratis Mesons haven't done much with their wealth, and a Gratis Meson just showed me one of the most innovative tools for peacekeeping I have ever seen. This will save a lot of lives." Sarah said out of genuine respect and admiration.

DeAmato smiled.

"There is so much more to come, my dear." He said.

DeAmato placed his hand on the door, and for the first time she noticed his GMA ring.

Sarah sat in the car and rested her head on the seat, closed her eyes and thought about Jade. He was right. He was the one who told her to listen to anyone wearing that ring, and she did. She missed Jade and longed to see him again.

*"For we must all appear before the judgment seat of Christ, so that each one may receive what is due for what he has done in the body, whether good or evil."*
*2 Corinthians 5:10*

# Chapter Thirteen

## The Past

Jade opened a card from Sarah. Inside was a note.

*Jade,*

*I just wanted to thank you for the wonderful night we had and for the information you shared with me. I know I have only known you for a few weeks, but you have inspired me. When we last spoke, I was all out of ideas; now, for the past two weeks, I have been diligently working on a winning proposal; all because I listened to you. Enclosed is something for you to remember me by.*

*With love,*
*Sarah*

*P.S: I hope you can take a hint… (See the back)*

Enclosed was a picture of Sarah. On the back was her address. Jade chuckled. The picture looked like it was a couple years old. Her hair was different. Her hair was dark, long, and curly. Sarah had since cut, straightened and lightened her hair, and she rarely wore it down. She looked so carefree and happy in the picture.

There was something about her that continued to captivate him, and the picture brought something back for Jade. Suddenly, like a bolt of lightning, memories began flowing, flashes of a woman—a woman who resembled Sarah in every important facet. The picture fluttered to the ground as Jade's grip on it failed him.

***

Jade was a rich Spaniard during the latter part of the 16th century living in England. He made a name for himself in Spain as an explorer and acquired much wealth and success on his own—but needed to marry well in order to have the societal clout that he desired. He already carried himself like a gentleman, and many high society women flocked to be in his presence.

Elisabeth had the perfect combination of beauty, wealth and standing. Jade pursued her with the same single-mindedness with which he sought the riches of the Americas, and took her hand in much the same way.

Jade and his wife acquired a large mansion with several acres of land. The two had many workers charged with the duty of maintaining the property. There was one chambermaid in particular who caught Jade's eye. Her name was Isabel. Her family worked for Elisabeth's family for many years, and Isabel was Elisabeth's favorite servant and friend.

Jade would watch her while she cleaned or scrubbed clothes outside. Sometimes she would look up and catch him peering out of a window. Jade was fascinated by Isabel and made his move. The two began an intense affair.

Jade would get up in the middle of the night, lean over, and kiss his wife.

"My love, I am going to the library."

Half asleep, Elisabeth would nod and quickly fall back into a deep slumber. Jade would wear a long black cloak and walk down to the basement. Isabel's room was at the end of a long corridor.

He would spend several hours in her room. They would make love and talk. Jade admired her exotic look and would always twist and play with her long black hair. Her skin was a deep brown, and her eyes were even deeper. Though she was one of the most beautiful women he had ever seen, her look was not favored by societal standards. She was colored. Jade had been many places in his life, seen distant lands, and he loved women who were different. Jade knew much of his success was attributed to his fair skin, which he resented at times. Jade took as many opportunities as he could to tell Isabel she was beautiful. He could tell that she had not heard that much in her life. Jade loved Isabel. He laughed more with her than with anyone else and she was the only one he could confide in. They only showed each other love at night, never during the day.

One day, Isabel entered the day room where Jade was hosting a meeting for a few statesmen.

"Jade, people have been talking about the name you have been making for yourself since you arrived in England. A few of us have some plans for you, if you are interested." A statesman said.

Jade smiled, knowing what this meant. He looked up and Isabel was standing in the corner staring at him. Jade stood up.

"Gentlemen, would you care for another drink?"

A few nodded. "Please continue, I must excuse myself."

He approached Isabel and began telling her what drinks to bring. He walked out of the room with her and quickly changed the conversation.

"What are you doing, Isabel? It is completely inappropriate to be in the room when gentlemen are talking." Jade whispered.

"I am with child…" Isabel replied.

Jade stepped back.

"What?"

"I am carrying your child." Isabel stated again.

Jade quickly looked around to see if anyone was within hearing distance.

"We will talk about this later."

Isabel nodded and continued her work. Although her predicament worried her, she trusted Jade more than anyone in the world.

***

That night Jade stayed in his bed. He did not go to see her. The next day he continued to ignore and avoid Isabel. Jade continued this behavior for weeks until one day, Jade was about to get into the carriage with his wife when Isabel started marching towards him. Jade saw her, she looked angry. He calmly continued into the carriage when Isabel grabbed his arm.

"I need to speak with you, sir!"

Elisabeth looked worried.

"What is it Isabel?" She asked.

Isabel eyed Jade who looked increasingly angered. Isabel quickly made up a lie.

"Sir Walter wanted to speak with you before you went into town…"

"I had already spoken to Sir Walter," Jade replied. "Please make certain never to grab the arm of a statesman with such authority. Know your station, girl!"

Isabel was completely embarrassed. She stood there sadly and watched as Jade's carriage head down the road.

That night Jade visited her. She merely cracked open the door.

"What do you want, sir?"

Jade aggressively pushed open the door and grabbed Isabel by the arms.

"What the HELL is your problem? Are you trying to destroy ME?"

Isabel broke free and screamed.

"You have not spoken to me in a month! Do you even care?" Jade calmed her down, suddenly aware of their excessive volume.

"Of course, I care. You know my situation. I have a wife, Isabel!" Jade whispered.

"A wife you have no love for!" Isabel retorted.

"Listen, if I could, I would be with you. However, things are not that way. You know what you have to do…"

Isabel looked up at Jade and with watering eyes screamed.

"NO! I am not getting rid of my baby!"

"Isabel you have no choice!" Jade said authoritatively.

"I will just leave then; I will run away! You would not care." Isabel said.

"You have nowhere to go; Elisabeth would be heartbroken."

Isabel understood all too well what type of man Jade was now.

"I do not care if I have a boy and he looks just like you! I am having my child. You do not have to speak to me again from this point." Isabel opened the door, and Jade walked out.

Jade understood people were not stupid. Jade also knew that it would only be a matter of time before Isabel started talking. After the scene she made, there could only be more emotional displays in store.

***

Jade confided in Sir Walter, who was his best friend and at times, a man of questionable character.

"You have a lot to lose with this wench." Walter said.

"I do love her. I created this situation, and I have to face it; there is no other way." Jade replied.

Walter cautiously offered an alternative solution.

"I have associates who have the means to take care of the situation for you." Walter said.

Jade, whose head was buried in his hands, quickly lifted his head and eyed Walter with a disturbed look on his face.

"What do you mean? Are you suggesting—"

"Everything will be fine. Think about it for a moment: Do you really want a bastard who looks just like you working in your home? I will take care of everything. After tonight, you will not have to think about it again." Walter said.

Jade paused for a moment to think about the decision he was about to make. Walter looked at him and smiled.

Sir Walter wrote a number on a piece of paper and slid it across the table. "Just give me that amount, and I'll take care of everything. Jade reached into his coat and fingered the bag of coins he kept on him at all times—just for emergencies. He retrieved the red velvet bag and dropped it into Walter's hand. The coins jumbled over themselves, making an ungodly noise that seemed louder and more final than any sound Jade had ever heard before.

***

Days turned into weeks, and weeks turned into months. Jade had not seen Isabel. His wife constantly asked about her and was deeply saddened by her disappearance.

"Why would she just leave like this, Jade? We treated her well, did we not?" Elisabeth wondered aloud.

It was highly uncommon for servants to just leave, but that was the only explanation he could offer his wife.

***

Jade saw Walter at a party and it was evident he had too much to drink.

"How is the *statesman* doing?" Walter yelled from across the room.

Jade had not spoken to Walter in months—since the transaction. Jade pulled Walter to the side.

"Where is Isabel? I need to know she is in good keeping. I want to be certain of this." Jade said. Walter snorted, rancid-smelling wine sputtering out of his mouth and stuck to his threadbare mustache.

"When you asked if she would be okay, I told you, that *you* would be okay… And that seemed to be well enough for you." Walter continued to laugh. Jade grabbed Walter by the collar.

"Get yourself together, man! What happened to her?" Jade said.

Walter ripped himself from Jade's grasp.

"Well, I can tell it is important for you to live in a state of denial; therefore, I am going to offer two scenarios. The first, after being told never to contact you again, she had a son and now cleans houses in town. Option two; five thugs had their way with her, before cutting her throat." Walter said.

Jade stumbled backward, groping for a surface. He found a chair and fell.

"I did not want this—I just wanted her gone."

Walter smiled at him.

"Chap, whom are you trying to convince? Yourself? You did not care more about her than you cared about yourself. Compared to yours, her life was meaningless, was it not? Think about it: is the world really so much the worse without her? Can the country not do without another servant to hem dresses, and tighten corsets, and spill the drinks? You had too much to lose." Walter said.

Jade composed himself, looked in the mirror for a long time, then abruptly dusted himself off.

"You are right, Walter. She was just a servant who was determined to bring me down. I have worked too hard to get here just to give it all up, for what—? Who would not have done what I had?" Jade asked, hoping for the reassurance he knew Walter would eagerly give him.

"What is important now is to forget about her and move on. No one will ever find out…" Walter stood behind Jade, placed both hands on his shoulders, and smiled. Jade never spoke or thought of Isabel from that day forward.

***

After reflecting, Jade knew Walter was a demon. Walter was the one who persuaded him to make the decision that made him lose his salvation. For the first time in centuries, Jade's eyes watered as he realized how easily he had been duped. He could feel himself getting weaker. The despair Azul warned him about was beginning to set in. Jade was intelligent enough to understand that all reminders of his past life and the decisions that led him to Hell had to be eliminated. Jade picked up the picture and gazed at her once more. His anger grew more intense as his hand involuntarily crumpled the picture of Sarah.

*"So we do not lose heart. Though our outer self is wasting away, our inner self is being renewed day by day." 2 Corinthians 4:16*

# Chapter Fourteen

## Re-Focus

Steven missed heaven more each day. At times it was difficult to continue his mission. The environment alone was seeping in and corrupting his thoughts, but he knew the importance of pressing on. It seemed like everywhere he turned, he saw demons, and the thought of continually having to walk amongst them sickened him. He had not even been on earth very long and already encountered sin and death. Ironically, he had not even met Sarah, and his resolve was dwindling. Steven knew his meeting with Carlos was not happenstance. It had to be a part of God's plan. His family reinforced for him that people were hopeful and maintained a strong sense of faith during the most desperate situations. Steven now understood the smallest amount of faith was something he could work with. However, Steven had full awareness that keeping faith was an ongoing struggle living in the devil's domain. The constant barrage of thoughts and temptations available to lead humans away from God were boundless and protecting their souls against sin would be an endless battle. Steven needed to refocus on his mission. Carlos was nice enough to help Steven locate Sarah.

"Thank you for staying with us. It really meant a lot to me and my mom." Carlos said.

"Thank you for being so kind. You helped me more than you will ever know." Steven replied as he rested his hand on the boy's shoulder and pulled him into his arms.

For Carlos, it was difficult to pull away. This stranger showed him more kindness than most of his family. Though Carlos knew he would never see Steven again, he would remember his kindness throughout his lifetime.

Steven arrived outside of Sarah's building. He suddenly realized that he had not developed a plan on how he would approach her. Steven assumed that once he introduced himself to her, she would have some willingness to converse with him. That is what occurred with Carlos. Steven hadn't considered exactly how much the people on Earth valued outward appearances. Even though he was clean, he found mismatched clothes from a church donation box. As soon as he entered the main lobby, several people stared at him like he did not belong.

"Hello, I am here to see Sarah Michel, is she available?" Steven asked politely.

The front desk concierge eyed Steven up and down.

"And how do you know Ms. Michel?"

"I am an old friend of hers." Steven replied.

"Just a moment—I'll see if she is available."

Just then, an elevator door slid open on the other side of the lobby. Steven could feel it was her even before she emerged, clutching a cell phone to her ear. Steven approached her cautiously.

"Sarah..." Steven made sure his voice was loud enough to hear.

Sarah flinched. She studied him from head to toe, and her lip curled into a sneer of disgust. He was dark brown, slender and tall, bushy hair, with a small goatee. He had the strangest tie-dyed shirt and questionably-tight tan pants that did not reach his ankles. Sarah thought he could be attractive, if not for his choice of attire.

"Who are you?" she demanded as she recoiled a step.

"Sarah, I need to talk to you. It is very important." Steven said as he reached for her hand.

Before his fingertips touched her hand, a burly security guard had his hands clasped around Steven's shoulders, restraining him.

"Do you know this gentleman?" The guard asked.

"Of course not!" Sarah yelled, "Isn't it obvious he's homeless?"

The guards lifted Steven up and escorted him outside.

"Sir, you are not allowed on the premises without the direct approval of Ms. Michel."

Steven wondered how he would be able to get close to her. How could he even hope Sarah would listen if he never had an opportunity to talk with her? Steven saw Sarah get in a town car. He flagged down a cab and followed.

*"See, I have set before you today life and good, death and evil." Deuteronomy 30:15*

# Chapter Fifteen

## Hidden Agenda

When Sarah got to the office, Shiloh handed her a package.

"This was delivered for you this morning."

Sarah went into her office and closed the door. She opened the package and there was another packaged sealed inside with a folded letter. A small disc fell out. On the outside it said, "Watch later." Sarah placed it in her desk and read the letter:

*Dear Ms. Michel,*

*The enclosed images are top secret files taken from Future Intellect, Inc. If you want to know what this is all about, call the number on the back of this letter.*

Sarah was disturbed, but opened the package anyway. There were hideous images of dismembered bodies. Then, there was a single photograph of a few scientists and what looked like

DeAmato standing by a medium sized sphere. Sarah thought it was a sick joke, but maintained her composure.

"Sally, who brought this package here?" Sarah asked angrily.

"He said he was from Future Intellect, and if you had any questions just to call the number inside. He was very polite." Shiloh replied.

Sarah closed the door and called the number.

"Ms. Michel, I was expecting your call."

"Listen, you freak, if you are trying to play games—"

"I assure you Ms. Michel, this is not a game."

The gentleman gave her the meeting location and Sarah immediately left the office.

***

Sarah arrived at a rundown motel off a highway in Southern Maryland. She was slightly afraid; but somehow, fear could not prevent her from finding out what was going on with her proposal. She knocked on door 154, and it opened. Standing in the doorway was the strange Indian man from the Future Intellect presentation.

"Please come in." he said.

Sarah stepped in cautiously and took a seat at the table.

"My name is Bartesh, and I am a lead engineer for Future Intellect. I specialize in Thermodynamics."

"What the hell is this about?" Sarah said as she slid the photos across the table.

"Ms. Michel, this is what Future Intellect, Inc. really does…"

Just then, a small Korean gentleman walked out of the bathroom.

"This is Daniel. He's the one who took these pictures. He works in the Special Environmental Services Department. That's a fancy way of saying housekeeping. It's the type of 'housekeeping' he does that makes what I'm about to tell you scary." Bartesh said.

"So, are you telling me this company is somehow involved in the murder of these people? Why? How?"

Bartesh pulled his chair closer to Sarah and began to speak.

"I know it's really hard to wrap your mind around. I felt the same way just a few months ago when Daniel showed me those pictures. The prototype you saw in the presentation is only one of the inventions we've been working on. My company is really involved in a much more controversial business—war weapons.

"Wait, what? War weapons? I don't believe this. If this were true, how could you not know?" Sarah asked.

"You have to understand the culture of Future Intellect." Bartesh said. "This company sells itself as a think tank and recruits the greatest minds from around the world. They offer young scientists and engineers six-figure salaries to sit around in a state-of-the-art lab, with everything we could possibly need at our fingertips, and then tell us to ponder the impossible. Our only job is to contemplate realistic ways to make it all possible. There are huge incentives for doing so: luxurious vacations and insane bonuses. We never took the time to think about the moral and ethical implications of what we did. To us, we were just a bunch of geeks doing what we loved: solving problems. Everything at Future Intellect is separated. The idea guys are separate from the builders. The builders are separate from the testers. And no one has any idea how management plans to use the final product. The company places designers on teams and encourages a feverishly competitive environment. It had gotten so competitive that we'd view our colleagues on different teams like our enemies. Looking back, it was a brilliant company strategy, and as smart as we all were, we bought it. We didn't consider what we were creating— honestly, we didn't care. If it was a weapon, it just had to be more diabolical than anything the other team could theorize. Basically, if you had our weaponry, you'd win. Period. A few years ago, they charged my team with the task of designing a weapon that was less devastating on the environment, but still had the capability of a massive kill. After thinking for months, we thought it best to move from explosives all together. We know that at about 125 degrees Fahrenheit your muscles will start to melt. And around 130 degrees Fahrenheit the human body can actually liquefy. To melt steel, often used in the structural framework of buildings, heat must be at least 2750 degrees Fahrenheit. Also, concrete requires thousands of degrees to crumble and break apart. Conceivably, a laser heated to a certain point could easily slice through human tissue and muscle, but would not be hot enough to cause real damage to buildings and other property. Lasers are used to cut in medicine all the time, why not weapons? The weapon we created was the Annihilator. It's a sphere that can be controlled remotely and hovers—similar to that of drone technology. It's not very big, but it doesn't have to be. The weapon is porous around the center of its body and emits extremely hot laser energy. Once the Annihilator is placed in a small city or town, there's no escape. The ball will disperse the heated laser and will spin rapidly, slicing everything in its path. The worst part is the sphere releases a pheromone that paralyzes a person for 15 minutes, leaving them unable to run. Then it goes to work."

Sarah was puzzled.

"So the same technology in the presentation given is the same technology used in this weapon?"

"Yes…"

"What do you want me to do? Why are you telling me all of this?" Sarah said.

"Your company is one of the most recognized in the world. Your company will legitimatize the work that is being done here, plus give us the funding needed to continue building the weapon. What DeAmato failed to tell you is a year ago we began meeting with government officials in France and Britain to see if the Crime Halter could be implemented by their police and military forces. Information about the device was leaked, and several advocacy groups questioned the ethical use of this device on civilians. But this discussion has gone under the radar. Only a few independent news outlets have reported on it. Needless to say, DeAmato is racing against time. He needs the backing of a well-known company that works closely with the U.S. Government to legitimize and mass produce the Crime Halter. DeAmato has funded the research and design of the Crime Halter and the Annihilator himself, but would go broke mass producing it. Once he has revenue from this device, research will continue on the Annihilator—the prototype is in its third phase of production. DeAmato is willing to sell this weapon to the highest bidder. He could care less who gets it or what this weapon will do. I have been stalling for the past year on the final step. He wants the laser to extend for at least 10 miles. I have capped the laser at 1.5 miles. But the technology is there for the beam to be longer. It's only a matter of time before he replaces me on the project and finds someone who will figure out how to do it faster."

Sarah was overwhelmed by the information she was hearing. She continued to look at the pictures of the people who were dismembered and then the smiling face of DeAmato, and selfishly wondered why it had to be her that had to deal with this information.

Bartesh assumed she felt the way he once did when he learned the truth.

"I was like you." Bartesh confessed. "I was happy not knowing anything that was going on. I was just proud of the work that my team completed. We were inventors. We were problem solvers, and we were going to be rich. We weren't politicians, legislators, or philosophers—we were scientists. Our responsibility started with a question and ended with finding the answer. It wasn't our job to think about how our creation would be used. Like a knife cuts through bread, it can also cut a throat. Should we not create a knife because it has the potential to hurt someone? This reasoning did not make sense to me. I told myself the Annihilator would help us win wars and preserve the freedom our enemies threatened every day. That's how I lived with myself until Daniel found me in the parking garage of our building. We'd worked for the same company for years and never met, he just knew I was an engineer by my badge. When he showed me the pictures and told me what his job duties were, I couldn't believe it. I felt sick to my stomach. I resisted the notion for a while, but I knew I had to make a decision. I was accountable."

"I have to go to the bathroom for a second and compose myself." Sarah said.

She stepped into the bathroom and began washing her face. She stared in the mirror. This was too big for her. She was just one person. She would not be able to stop DeAmato. He was so well connected he'd ultimately get what he wanted. In the process he'd discredit her. He'd say Bartesh and his team acted alone. He'd find a way out. In the end, she'd just be like every other person who tried to take a stand: she'd lose everything and still nothing would change.

Suddenly, she heard loud knocking at the front door. She heard a voice she didn't recognize and Bartesh reply, "There's no one else here." She heard two muffled gunshots and the ruffling of paper. Sarah stayed quiet but heard the voice say, "Check the bathroom."

Sarah panicked as she struggled to lift the window. She used all of her strength, but the window wouldn't budge. She could see the doorknob jiggle and then the door shook violently. The window finally opened, giving her just enough time to wiggle out of the tiny space before the man kicked the door in. Sarah ran. She screamed when she turned back to see two men in all black chasing her. One of the men shot at her and missed. Sarah made a sharp turn down an alley and Steven, who had been following her all evening, ran in her direction. He tackled Sarah to the ground and pulled her behind a dumpster. He covered her mouth. She was breathing heavily as she tried to free herself from the hold he had. He removed his hand.

"Don't scream! I'm Steven. I saw you earlier, and I followed you here. Please be calm. You can trust me. "

Steven let her go and turned his back to her momentarily to

see if the men were close. When he turned around, Sarah had bolted in the other direction. He stood up and ran after her. The two men cut her off. One of the men grabbed her and punched her in the stomach and face rendering her unconscious. The other man pulled out a gun and pointed it at her head. He was about to pull the trigger when Steven rushed him, taking him to the ground. The weapon slid across the pavement. The other man pointed his gun at Steven, who was wrestling with the man's partner on the ground. The man with the gun waited for a clean shot. Steven, struggling to shield his body, screamed at the top of his lungs, "GOD HELP US!"

With a bolt of lightning, Josiah shook the ground upon entry. The impact created a violent quake that forced the gunman to his knees. As he struggled to regain his footing, the gunman fired several shots as Josiah approached but to no avail. No bullets could penetrate his heavenly armor. Josiah grabbed the gunman by the neck and lifted him high into the air. His heavy muscular build provided no resistance against the supernatural strength of the angel. Josiah effortlessly slammed his stocky frame into the concrete below—shattering the pavement surrounding his body. Frightened by what he saw, the other man ran as fast as he could away from Josiah. Without warning, Josiah spread his massive, majestic wings and took to the air. In shock and awe the man grew horrified as Josiah flew overhead. Transfixed on the angelic figure above him, the man ran into oncoming traffic and was killed instantly. Josiah swooped back over to Steven who was lying there helplessly.

"Are you ok? Jesus sent me to protect you."

Josiah looked at Sarah who was still unconscious, then looked at Steven who was quivering. Josiah had an immediate sense of how challenging Steven's mission would be.

"I will pray for you my brother." He whispered.

Josiah heard sirens. He expanded his wings and just as fast as he arrived, shot back into the sky.

*"If your right eye causes you to sin, tear it out and throw it away. For it is better that you lose one of your members than that your whole body be thrown into hell. And if your right hand causes you to sin, cut it off and throw it away. For it is better that you lose one of your members than that your whole body go into hell." Matthew 5:29-30*

# Chapter Sixteen

## Black or White

When Sarah opened her eyes, she was in a hospital bed with an IV in her arm. She could not recall much of anything. She was weak but managed to sit up. Steven was sleeping uncomfortably in the chair next to her. Sarah looked at him and tried to figure out how he fit into all of this. Steven's eyes opened and he saw Sarah quietly looking at him.

"You're awake." Steven said.

"Who are you?" Sarah asked as a sharp pain shot through her jaw.

"My name is Steven. Three days ago, you were attacked. I was there and intervened."

Sarah remembered. She was chased and beaten after she

was given information from Bartesh. A nurse walked in and saw that she was up and took her temperature.

"How are you feeling?" the nurse asked.

Sarah nodded slowly.

"Well, if you are up to it, two detectives are here to see you." The nurse said.

As the detectives walked in, Sarah became uncomfortable and felt unprepared.

"Hi, Ms. Michel. I am Detective Ransome and this is Detective Staller, we just want to ask you a few questions about what happened a few days ago."

Sarah nodded, and the detectives took seats.

"Well, Ms. Michel three people are dead. One is paralyzed, and the motel where you were last seen caught on fire. Could you help us piece together exactly what happened? Why were you in a motel so far outside of D.C. anyway?"

Sarah lied: "Well… I was meeting up with… Steven, just to get out of the city, when I was attacked by two men. I was knocked out… I don't remember too much after that."

The detective looked suspiciously at Sarah, and then turned to Steven. "Could you corroborate this?"

Steven looked back at Sarah who put him in a very uncomfortable position. He also didn't exactly lie—but did practice careful omission.

"Yes, we were meeting up, and I saw two men chase her. I tried fighting them off when another man came to our defense, but I could not see his face."

"Was this man an *Angel?*" the detective asked.

Steven's heart dropped, shocked that he would even know to ask the question.

"What do you mean?" Steven asked.

"Well, one of your attackers, who is now paralyzed, was admitted to the Psych ward after continually ranting about an angel breaking his back. He had no identification, and he has been incoherent for a while." The detectives chuckled to themselves, then handed a card to Sarah.

"If you remember anything else, give us a call. We are continuing this investigation." the detective said as he tipped his hat and followed his partner out the door.

"Why were you really at the motel?" Steven asked, angered that she incorporated him into her lie.

"I'm tired…" Sarah replied.

Steven grabbed her by the shoulder, forcing her to face him.

"Why did you lie?" Steven asked again.

Sarah just looked at him. She knew now that these people were dangerous. The last thing she wanted was police involvement.

***

Over the next couple of days Steven and Sarah bonded. She wondered why he seemed so dedicated to her, but she was glad he was around because she had no one else.

Sarah's cell phone rang several times. It was her mother. Steven gave her the phone, but she shook her head.

"Just turn the phone off." Sarah said.

"You don't want to tell your mother how you're doing? I'm sure she's worried." Steven replied.

Sarah's eyes were half closed.

"The last thing I care about is my mother…" she said.

"How can you say that about your mother, Sarah?"

"I can say that because for years, she never cared about herself and certainly not me!" Sarah's eyes began to water rather easily just talking about her mother. "You have no idea what I have been through, and just because she has the title 'mother' doesn't make her a good one."

Steven wanted to delve further, but thought it would be best to leave it alone for now. To his surprise Sarah voluntarily continued.

"She would have been eleven …" Sarah mumbled as her

eyes turned toward the window.

"What do you mean?" Steven asked.

Sarah turned back to look at him and tears were streaming down her face.

"They're gone and it's her fault!"

In that moment, her mind traveled back eleven years. Sarah was a newlywed and was in her ninth month of pregnancy.

"I felt the contractions. It was time." She uttered reliving the moment.

"We had practiced the drill so many times. My husband, Thomas, normally would have been the driver, but he had broken his arm a few weeks prior and could not drive with the cast. So, we asked my mother, who swore to me that she had not been drinking that day, and there was no time to question her. We got in the car and were heading toward the hospital when she veered into oncoming traffic. It happened so quickly.

"Moments before, Thomas seated in the front, turned to me and held my hand as he cracked corny jokes to take my mind off the pain. A car hit us and sent our car spinning off the road down the hillside. He did not put on his seatbelt, because he complained that it made his arm feel even more restricted. I told him to put it on—he was always so stubborn! I remember crawling out of the car and saw blood everywhere. Blood soaked my white sweater and I prayed that it was my blood! I prayed that my baby was alive.

"When I finally reached the hospital, I was told that my child and my husband were gone, I begged Jesus to bring them back! My life no longer had purpose without them. Instead, like a sick joke, God allowed my mother—a drunk—to continue living. The worst part is that my mom only spent two years in jail. She stopped drinking and 'found' God again, but unfortunately, that does not bring back my unborn child and the love of my life. Now that she's a 'Holy Roller' she wants to be a mother after being absent for the majority of my life.

"As for God… He really has done nothing for me except

take away the only things that mattered, for what… A lesson? Was the death of my husband and child apart of that, 'everything happens for a reason' nonsense? Why is it that no one can ever figure out the reason?"

Steven was at a loss for words. Her question seemed rhetorical, but she appeared to be waiting for an answer. Steven was about to say something, but Sarah cut him off.

"The reason does not exist. If the loss of my child was a part of His bigger plan… I want no part of it."

Steven was deeply saddened by her story and now saw how hopeless she was. Anger and pain ran deep in Sarah. She only cared about herself now because she believed "herself" was all she had. It was obvious she felt her mother and God had abandoned her. Steven normally would have prayed for guidance. But he did not. Instead, he held Sarah's hand tightly. He watched tears stream down her face and he gently wiped them away. Steven saw Sarah's eyes close and felt her slender hand grip tighter.

***

When they arrived at Sarah's apartment building, Steven was hesitant to set foot inside. He still had bruising from the tussle with the security guards. Sarah, sensing his discomfort, grabbed his hand and walked with him inside. Steven saw people eyeing him as they headed toward the elevators.

When they walked into Sarah's apartment, it was cold and drafty.

"I must have left a window open…"

Steven took a seat on the couch and waited patiently for Sarah. The home-phone rang and Sarah picked it up in her room.

"Hello…?" Sarah answered.

"Hi, Sarah I have called you and left several messages." DeAmato said.

Sarah felt very uneasy speaking with him, but calmly masked her fear.

"You were worried about me?" Sarah replied.

"Oh yes, Sarah. I attended two funerals this week… I did not want to attend another. I have noticed when people try to be heroes, death seems to find them… I hope you're not thinking about trying to be one?"

"Is that a threat, Mr. DeAmato?" Sarah asked.

"No, Sarah, of course not. It is merely an observation. Did you see the gift I left for you?"

"No…" Sarah said cautiously.

"It's on your bed." DeAmato replied.

Sarah was scared. DeAmato or one of his men had been in her apartment. She looked over and saw a "Get Well" card. Inside it read:

*Dear Sarah,*

*Get very well! Your presentation is in one week. Please do not let new information hinder you from making the presentation of your LIFE!*

Sarah closed the card.

"Thank you for the card…" Sarah said.

"No, thank you Ms. Michel for aggressively pitching our concept to your employers… I will make sure to attend the presentation and provide you with all the motivation needed to execute a flawless delivery."

Sarah slammed the phone down.

"Damn it!" She screamed.

Steven rushed into her room.

"What's going on?" Steven asked with concern in his voice.

Sarah prided herself on being smarter than most, with an innate ability to figure things out on her own. She could always find that gray area, no matter how small, that left both sides pleased, or at the very least left her without blame. Secretly, this is how she climbed the corporate ladder, by managing never to offend anyone that mattered, even in the most delicate circumstances. But the situation she found herself in had no gray area. It was black or white. A side had to be chosen. She needed to know what someone else would do in her position.

"Yeah, yeah… I'm fine…" Sarah said as she glanced at him.

"Have you ever been in a position where you are unsure of the right thing to do?" she asked.

"Well, the right thing to do should be obvious unless there is something else standing in the way." Steven said.

"What if your life is what is in the way of the right decision? What if your life is in the balance?" Sarah asked.

Steven pulled away and looked deep into her eyes.

"Are you faced with that decision now?" Steven asked.

Sarah's eyes began to water, and she hugged him. Steven held her and noticed her breathing heavily.

"I don't know what is up or down anymore, Steven; the only things that are real are the things in front of me."

Sarah didn't understand friendship with a man. Eventually, most of her male relationships turned sexual.

Sarah began kissing Steven. Steven was caught completely off guard and was defenseless against her advances. He was undeniably attracted to her, and upon first seeing her, feelings of lust infiltrated his thoughts. Sarah removed her shirt and began to unbuckle Steven's pants. Steven was stuck in the moment and felt himself not wanting to resist. Sarah pushed him on the bed and straddled him. He seemed like he hadn't done this in a while and that turned Sarah on more. She moved his hands where she wanted them to be. Steven became more aggressive in the moment and started kissing Sarah's neck.

"I want you inside me…" Sarah whispered in his ear.

Suddenly Steven stopped.

"Wait… Wait… This can't happen!"

Steven knew that Sarah had equated sex with comfort. It was something she used to make herself feel better when she was unsure of what else to do. It was only an instant fix. Steven could not take advantage of Sarah in this way. The only thing she needed was God. Sarah looked at him and began to cry. Steven wrapped his arms around her and held her. That's all she needed. In that moment Sarah felt so loved. She rested her head on Steven's chest and thought of her husband. She felt safe. The two drifted off to sleep.

***

Steven woke up and Sarah was still resting peacefully on his chest. Images of Sarah's body and lips kept replaying in his mind. Suddenly Steven remembered his own salvation. Since he had been around Sarah, he had been out of contact with God, and lustful thoughts clouded his mind. He carefully moved himself from under her and knelt by the bed. He began fervently praying. He could not hear anything. He jumped up and looked out the window. Everyone looked like humans! He was worried. Before, he could not walk down the street without seeing at least one demon at every corner. Now he could see none! Steven realized he was lost. He became frantic and started sweating.

The sound of Steven pacing back and forth woke Sarah up. She saw him and was immediately frightened by his behavior. She just knew she had something to do with it.

"Is it me?" She asked apprehensively.

Steven grabbed Sarah by the arms and caressed her face.

"No, no, it's not you... You are beautiful! But I think I messed up!"

Sarah looked confused by Steven's statement, but felt compelled to cover her half naked body.

"Listen to me! If you never listen to anything in your life listen to this: God is REAL! He is so, so, REAL!" Steven sat beside her and held her hands. As he spoke, each word sounded like he was going to cry.

"The life of your child and your husband was never yours, but His. You and I are His... EVERYTHING is His. Everything we are is rooted in Him and everything we do should be for the glory of Him!"

Sarah clung to every word. She had never seen anyone so passionate about his faith. This was different. Steven spoke like a man who had done more than studied, or listened, or researched... He spoke like a man who had personal knowledge. He spoke with such confidence and conviction that there was no debating. There were no alternative perspectives. No opinions... Just listening.

Steven began to look around at Sarah's neat room and all of her things. He seemed angry.

"None of this matters! None of it! This stuff you have— these things you have gathered... It's all worthless. Tell me Sarah, what's more valuable: having everything you could ever want, or having the only thing you need?"

Sarah, still quiet, suddenly felt ashamed. She had taken such pride in everything that surrounded her. Steven's speech made her feel so stupid.

"Don't you get it? It's kind of like God has given us all a ticket. He told us to hold on to that ticket. He showed us how to protect that ticket and even how to restore a damaged ticket. Then he told us that we all will need that ticket. But many of us have already traded the ticket for everything we could ever want. The time is coming when each one of us will need to stand before God and present that ticket. That ticket is the ONLY currency accepted to enter the ONLY place that ever mattered. So Sarah... Where's your ticket?"

Sarah wasn't expecting that question. She was stuck. Unsure if anything he'd said made sense to her, Steven crouched down to the floor and wept. "I failed you Father!" Steven uttered.

Sarah cried too and wanted to comfort him. She instinctively wrapped her arms around his shoulders and thought about everything he said, and the image of the ticket kept circling her mind.

Steven smelled her sweet perfume and for a moment, relished in the comfort she provided. If he had been praying and listening to Jesus, he would have known exactly what to tell Sarah that would lead her to the right decision. Steven figured he probably appeared to be a mad religious zealot in her eyes, and her heart was probably closed to his words now. He quickly pulled away from her, understanding now his *own* Salvation was in Jeopardy. He offered the last bit of advice his heart could muster.

"Whenever you are in doubt, or in danger, just call on Jesus. He will help you to see and hear truth when you need clarity."

Steven opened the front door and Jade was standing there. Steven and Jade stared at each other for about a minute. Steven was unaware of Jade's true nature. He could not see. Steven turned back toward Sarah.

"Please remember to call on Him. We are in spiritual warfare."

Steven rushed out the door and down the hall. Jade watched him and listened. And wondered why he would say, "spiritual warfare?" For Jade, it was a very odd thing for a human to say. Was he like Azul? He pondered.

Jade etched his face in his mind before noticing Sarah crying uncontrollably.

"Sarah, are you okay?" Jade asked.

"Jade, I'm lost… My faith in God used to be so strong. A man who showed me the most kindness and protection I've felt since my husband passed just ran out the door because he felt less connected to God for just a moment. And here I am questioning if God is real? Why?" Sarah begged him for any answer.

Jade looked at Sarah and needed to say exactly the right thing to keep her mind off of God. Jade decided to manipulate her sense of reason without being too obvious about his true intent.

"Sarah, I don't think there is a God." Jade said. "When we die, there is probably nothing. We will rot away in a pine box, and our bodies will become one with the soil. And guess what? That's alright." Jade wiped Sarah's eyes and made sure she was listening.

"All that we can focus on in this life is making every moment count. Why not be happy? Why not be with the person who makes you smile? Why not act on a physical connection you feel with someone? Why? Because a book says you can't? You only have one chance to live; why waste it following someone else's rules? This is your life! You make the rules! You decide how it ends. Really think about it Sarah, you're a smart woman. Does that make sense?"

"I don't know! What you said sounds right, but… but it doesn't feel right. I might need to pray. I haven't prayed in so long." Sarah said.

Jade became agitated. This was not at all what he wanted her to do.

"Listen, I'm here, I'll make you feel a lot better than any prayer would."

Jade lifted her off the ground and kissed her. The strangest feeling came over Sarah. In Jade's arms she did not feel emotionally safe. She actually felt scared. She wasn't sure if she was scared of him, or just scared by everything that had happened. She just knew she needed to be alone with her thoughts.

"Jade, please stop. I just need to be by myself."

"What are you going to do?" Jade asked frankly.

"I'm just going to pray for a while."

Jade looked at her. "No, I'll stay." He said.

***

Sarah began to kneel. As Sarah inched toward the ground, Jade became more frustrated, but tried hard not to show it. He heard Sarah briefly ask for understanding and guidance. When Sarah stood up again, Jade was staring at her with disdain. She had never seen that look on his face before. He looked like he was cursing at her in his mind. Jade's presence made her feel awkward. She never had that feeling around him, even when they first met.

"What?" Sarah asked.

"Do you feel better… Now that you wasted five minutes of your life praying to nothing?" Jade said sarcastically.

Sarah felt offend by his demeanor and wondered why he cared so much.

"You don't know that God doesn't exist, so why are you so bothered by me believing His existence might be a possibility?" Sarah said as she approached him. Jade tried hard to maintain his composure. Since he had been on earth, he had never had a debate about God with any human.

"Listen, let's just drop it; you are clearly emotional…" Jade said.

She looked into his eyes, and for the first time, noticed how large and black his pupils were. There was something missing in his eyes. Everything about him was suddenly creepy.

Sarah, uneasy, showed Jade to the door.

"We had a fling, but I don't think this is going to work. We are just different people, I guess."

"It's that guy, isn't it?" Jade said.

"Steven? In a way… yes. He has opened my eyes to things that were hard for me to see."

"But he wasn't wearing a GMA ring. How important could he really be?"

"He doesn't care about the ring, and neither do I."

Jade could tell there was no persuading her. She was resolved; she did not want him there.

As Sarah's door shut in his face, Jade was determined to find Steven and eliminate him.

*"Ponder the path of your feet; then all your ways will be sure." Proverbs 4:26*

# Chapter Seventeen

## The Decision

A week passed. The day of the big presentation arrived. A few months ago, all that consumed Sarah was winning—beating David—but so much more had happened. There was a lot more at stake. Sarah understood and was prepared. Her decision was made.

Sarah walked into the office and greeted her assistant.

"Hi, Shiloh. Would you mind sending these packages for me today, please?"

Shiloh was shocked by her relaxed attitude and even more surprised Sarah said her actual name.

"Sure, Ms. Michel... Will do."

Shiloh carefully grabbed the three packages from Sarah's hands and placed them in her desk for safekeeping.

When Sarah walked into the boardroom, David was already there, seated next to his intern, Jamal. The African businessmen Sarah had seen before were also there smiling comfortably as they made polite conversation with David and Jamal. DeAmato was seated directly across from them. He leaned forward confidently and patted the seat adjacent to him, condescendingly, welcoming Sarah to the seat. Sarah felt her body cringe; however, she only displayed the utmost professionalism.

"How are you doing Ms. Michel?" DeAmato asked.

"I'm well." Sarah replied making no eye contact with him.

Once everyone arrived, the President opened with a brief welcome speech.

"I want to thank everyone for coming today. David and Sarah have been working very hard over the past few months on the proposals we are about to see. There is a lot of work and research that goes into making a proposal to a company such as ours, and as you know, today's proposals will determine who will be promoted to the senior position in the Mergers and Acquisitions Department. We are all very eager to hear what fresh ideas, our stars have found. David, would you like to begin?"

David stood up and was slightly nervous, but covered it well. He was overly prepared; Sarah knew it, but was not intimidated.

"Good morning everyone, and thank you for the kind introduction, Mr. President..." David neatly organized his notes on the podium as Jamal began the slideshow.

"We are living in times that require innovative ways to solve the growing energy crisis. We can no longer believe the earth's resources are infinite. Now is the time for a drastic shift. We must shift how we think; shift our extreme comfort level; and most importantly, sacrifice a little for the betterment of all. Now is the time for us to begin to work together, be creative, and find better ways to renew our energy. Please focus your attention on the screen." David said as the video began to play.

The video showed images of a small town with beautiful one-level homes. These homes had solar panels all around the houses, and every home had a small garden toward one side. Under these gardens were tanks for water storage. The town was green, and there were carousels for children to spin and play on around every corner. Additionally, there was a larger farm for growing produce and windmills off in the distance.

"This… is the future. This town is a model town in Tanzania that has been inhabited for a year by 250 persons displaced from genocide and war. Everything in this town is made out of recyclable materials, and the town only uses renewable energy sources. The homes are called Adobe homes, constructed from mud and other natural materials. All water used is recycled and purified through the groundwater filtering process in the garden. Waste accumulated from drains inside the homes is emptied into the garden. The water trickles down through the garden—cleaned by rocks and other natural minerals. The water drips through a micro filter, before it is stored in a tank. The water is able to be retrieved and used within the houses again. The carousals seen throughout the town double as water pumps for additional water storage. As the children spin the carousals, they are unknowingly executing the work of several men pumping water into tanks throughout the town. Researchers have done the tests, this town's carbon footprint is less than three mid-sized homes in the United States."

David went on to explain that nothing is left to waste in the town. People are taught to produce their own food to use only what is needed. Communities like these could be built all over the World. He explained that the cost to construct this environment would really be limited to labor. The builders get most of their materials from Recycling Plants and landfills.

"I have reached out to contacts in a few East African governments interested in funding these living environments once the studies from the model town are completed. Our company would design, construct, and maintain these communities."

David's proposal would make an impact. If the executives wanted "fresh ideas" David delivered. However, it was obvious: the return on investment for this project was not great.

"David, have you done any market research to see if

Americans would be interested in these kinds of living dwellings?" An executive asked.

"We have, sir, and the numbers are not favorable here. However, we would implement an excellent Public Relations campaign, should we decide to pursue building these homes here initially. The numbers show that these communities will produce high revenue overseas in underdeveloped regions. We are involved in every step of the process, the impression I have gathered, is that these governments are willing to step aside and allow us to spearhead the effort while they simply cut the check."

David received "looks" from the executives he had not expected and decided to speak candidly in a last-ditch effort to win them over.

"Money will be made from this project. I assure you. But more than that, we have seen what this environment can do for people. It has literally uplifted and empowered a group of people who had lost hope."

The executives scribbled in their pads.

"Are these homes intended for those living in poverty?" An executive asked.

David was frustrated by the question, but tried his best to make them understand.

"No, these homes are intended for those willing to reduce the harm they are causing to the environment on a daily basis. Yes, these homes will require that people learn to live modestly and within their means; however, it is a lesson I feel many will be able to apply to their lives rather quickly. The homes are no different from any one level house in America."

The executives thanked David for the presentation.

***

As Sarah prepared for her presentation, Steven was immersed in deep prayer and fasting.

He found a small church on the outskirts of the city upon

leaving Sarah's home franticly that evening. He had to find God.

The church was kind enough to offer him shelter while he centered himself once again. Steven was terrified of going back into the world without knowing he was saved. It had been several days, and the more he prayed the louder God's voice became. Initially, it was so faint. It sounded like there was nothing. Steven had to listen closely to hear God, and he did. Steven reclaimed his confidence and his spiritual strength. He was ready to reunite with Sarah once again. He stood up from the pew, respectfully made the sign of the cross and re-entered the harsh world.

***

Jade had been following Steven ever since that day. He waited patiently in the distance for him to leave the church. Jade was going to enjoy pushing Steven to his own demise. As Steven stepped outside, the cold sharply hit his face. The sky darkened and an ominous feeling overwhelmed his spirit. His senses were heightened once again. Steven raised his eyes forward and squinted. He could only make out two green dots. For fractions of a second, they would disappear like a blink. Were they eyes? Steven did not know. Then he heard panting, like the breathing of some kind of large animal. Sensing something was wrong, he felt the urge to run. But where?

Steven was blindsided, taken to the ground by a horrific creature that now sat upon his chest, scratching and tearing at his flesh with deadly intentions. Steven could sense that it was Jade, even without glimpsing his human form. Steven screamed and pulled out a crucifix. He mashed it into Jade's shoulder. The cross burned through several layers of skin. Jade howled in agony and was momentarily distracted. Steven scrambled to his feet and fled.

Jade returned to his human form and started throwing rocks and whatever objects were in arm's reach in Steven's direction. He averted the threats and took a sharp turn into the woods where he hid behind a large boulder. Steven tried hard not to make a sound.

***

Sarah stood up and took a moment to look around. She saw David who was attentive and respectful. Then she observed DeAmato's threatening eyes piercing through her. Sarah began.

"More than 65,000 police officers are assaulted annually, and more that 23,000 officers die every year. Why is this the case? In the instance when an officer must exit his vehicle after pulling over a suspect, he is in the most danger. He could be killed."

Sarah's eyes scanned the room and everyone was attentive. DeAmato grinned anxiously.

"Future Intellect, Inc. has developed a revolutionary device which will change how we fight crime forever." Sarah continued with the presentation.

***

Jade found Steven crouching in a ditch. He created a force that pulled Steven by the legs toward the edge of a steep cliff that overlooked a shallow creek. Steven felt his body lift and before he knew it, he was standing on the edge overlooking a canyon. Jade created a huge shield behind him. Steven could not turn back. He could only stay perfectly still or jump. One wrong move would send him plummeting to his death.

***

Sarah finished her presentation, and by the looks on their faces, she could tell it won the Executives' approval. The Executives scribbled in their pads and conversed briefly.

"Sarah, it is clear the Crime Halter will be our next investment. It is more aligned with our vision as a company. Your hard work earned you the position of Senior Corporate Executive in Mergers and Acquisitions."

The Executives stood up and shook her hand. David graciously congratulated her.

"Sarah, you gave an excellent presentation. Congrats! I look forward to your leadership." David said.

Sarah, despondent, continued to stand at the podium as people talked amongst themselves.

***

Steven could feel himself falling forward. Jade had to use every ounce of energy he had to hold the force field, but he was prepared to endure long enough for Steven to leap out in desperation. Steven had nowhere to go. There was no escape. Steven uncomfortably pressed his back against the clear wall Jade created, hoping his feet did not accidently slip. He was going to die before he had any time to make an impression on Sarah. The thought of disappointing God troubled him.

Suddenly, Steven's feet were no longer on the cliff's edge; his body was suspended in the air. He could feel himself floating higher and higher as the image of Jade got smaller and smaller. Steven continued to float into the sky, past the stratosphere, further into space, and higher up until once again he was in Heaven before the throne.

Steven could not look at Jesus. He kept his eyes down ashamed of what he had done while on earth. Ashamed he strayed away so much and God saw it all. Jesus approached Steven, raised him up and embraced him. Steven could only cry.

"Sarah made her choice, Steven." Jesus said. "That is why you have been called back."

Steven knew he failed his mission. He did not spend enough time with her. In the moments they shared, Steven had not been the best example of righteousness. In fact, his dealings with her that night probably left her more confused. Steven was immediately dismayed by this thought, but remained grateful he had not lost his Salvation.

"Why does your heart feel sadness?" God asked.

"I have disappointed you—I did not carry out my mission successfully." Steven replied.

"How are you so certain, my child?" God asked.

Steven was hesitant to confess.

"Father I have sinned…" he said. "I have sinned so much that I feel it hindered Sarah's ability to build her faith. At the moment, she may have been most willing to listen, I gave into temptation, and I believe I lost credibility with her."

There was a long pause. Then God spoke. "You did very well my child. You have earned your wings."

Steven looked toward God and was speechless. Sarah made the right choice.

***

Sarah watched everyone standing and talking.

"I'm not finished," She said authoritatively.

The Executives were stunned by her tone. She pulled several photographs out of her briefcase. They were the images Bartesh had given her. She held them up, and the group gasped. "This is what DeAmato wants." Sarah pointed to the image of the Annihilator.

"This weapon will cause catastrophic death and they have already tested it on people." Sarah said.

The group looked at DeAmato who coolly smirked at the accusation.

"Your proof is a few pictures that look like they could have been still-shots from any horror movie. How do I know they are real? You better come harder than that if you want to mess with me. My attorneys will rip you and this company apart and win!"

Sarah was relaxed as she pulled out a disk and inserted it into the laptop. A video of Bartesh appeared on the screen behind her.

"My name is Bartesh Alamar. I have been the lead engineer for Future Intellect, Inc. for approximately seven years. I cannot stand idle while these crimes continue."

After he spoke, there was video footage of Daniel picking up limbs and organs and placing them in large trash bags.

Suddenly the group saw the camera begin to shake violently. They saw Daniel's face in the frame adjusting the lens while a towel is thrown over the top of the camera without blocking the lens. The camera is now focused on the entrance door to the warehouse. They see DeAmato enter and begin coughing.

"Oh… This smell is putrid! How do you guys do it?" DeAmato says.

DeAmato walks out of the frame, and then quickly walks back. He examines the weapon.

"Are you sure this thing is off?" He says to the tech accompanying him. "I certainly wouldn't want to look like this guy!" DeAmato says jokingly as he kicks the man's chest.

The man on the floor was cut by the laser which severed his torso separating the lower half of his body from the top half. The man was still barely alive, and with the little life he had left, grabbed DeAmato's leg and begged him for help. DeAmato coldly pointed a gun at his head and shot three bullets. DeAmato looked at Daniel.

"Please dispose of these people properly and ensure they are dead! This has happened twice now, and it becomes rather irritating when they reach for me! Do you understand me?" the tape went black and then snowy.

The room fell silent. DeAmato aggressively approached Sarah. David stood in front of her.

"Whatever you're about to do is not a good idea. I suggest you leave…" David said. DeAmato noticed Jamal on the phone speaking quietly. DeAmato continued to stare at Sarah threateningly as he exited. Everyone was at a loss for words, unsure of what to say. Sarah broke the silence.

"I'm sorry, but I can't accept the position." Sarah said. "David is capable of handling all the duties associated with the senior management position. I just need get out of here."

Sarah grabbed her bag and walked out of the room. David followed behind.

"We needed to see that. You did the right thing Sarah."

David said.

Sarah looked defeated.

"What does that mean, David?" Sarah said as water welled in her eyes.

"It means doing the right thing will be the hardest thing you'll do, and it will cost you more than you planned, but it's worth it every single time."

Sarah smiled appreciatively at David and regrettably thought about the proposal of sharing the senior position he made in her office months ago. Nevertheless, what's done is done. Sarah affixed her eyes forward and continued walking. David gazed at her as she walked down the hallway. That would be the last time he'd see Sarah.

***

When DeAmato reached the lobby, he saw several police officers run past him. He hid his face and flagged a cab down outside. He jumped in and immediately called Samuel Linden, "We have a problem…"

*"And whenever you stand praying, forgive, if you have anything against anyone, so that your Father also who is in heaven may forgive you your trespasses."*
*Mark 11:25*

# Chapter Eighteen

## Home

Sarah arrived at the front door and paused for several moments. She inhaled deeply before she knocked. She heard nothing and quickly turned away.

A voice said, "Just a moment…"

The door opened.

"Sarah…?"

Sarah's back was turned. She closed her eyes tightly and looked back over her shoulder and nodded. Her mother, without hesitation, stretched her arms to embrace Sarah. She had not seen her daughter in years. Her mother held her with the same intensity as finding a lost child.

She looked the same. Her hair had grown more silver. She even smelled the same—like cinnamon and sugar, just as Sarah remembered. Sarah always loved that smell and longed for it many years ago when her mother only smelled of alcohol.

As Sarah walked in, she looked around with amazement. The house looked so much nicer than she remembered. It felt like home. For years, she never was able to create that feeling in her apartment.

Her mother had pictures with children she taught at her church. It seemed like she truly rebuilt her life.

"I prayed for this day for the longest time." Her mother said as she continued cooking in the kitchen.

Sarah was still very quiet as she took everything in. She saw a picture of her mother with a handsome older man.

"Who is he?"

Without seeing, her mother knew whom Sarah was referencing.

"That's my husband, John."

Sarah was stunned. It was the death of her father that drove her mother to drink in the first place. Her mother was so depressed and withdrawn. Sarah believed there was no way she would ever move on.

"We met at church, and he has been so supportive and understanding. He truly is heaven sent." Her mother said.

Sarah could not hide the fact that it seemed her mother had easily moved on after the death of her grandchild and son-in-law.

"Mom, do you ever think about them?" Sarah asked.

Her mom stopped what she was doing and stepped out of the kitchen. She opened the pendent hanging on the necklace she was wearing. It was a picture of a pregnant Sarah and her husband.

"Every day for the past 11 years. I know God has forgiven me for the two lives I carelessly took, but your forgiveness was never promised to me. Forgiving me has been a decision you have had to make. I wanted you to forgive me, not for my sake, but for your own. Having hatred in your heart is how you will be held accountable for the loss of your husband and child. Forgiveness is hard, especially when you know the pain will never quite go away.

I prayed that if I ever had the opportunity to see you again, I would show you the power of forgiveness."

Her mother opened a photo album of pictures taken while she worked in a special prison rehabilitation program. The program allowed inmates to face the families of their victims.

"A man high on drugs broke into a house while the family's teenage son was home alone. Thinking no one was home, he was startled by a noise. Without thinking, he turned and shot at the noise repeatedly. The first shot instantly killed the boy. The man was apprehended and sentenced to life in prison. For years, he wanted to apologize, and for years, I regrettably delivered the same news: the family did not want to see him.

"Eventually, the inmate gave up, and I no longer received a request from him. One day, out of the blue, the family called and requested a meeting with him. The inmate had now grown apprehensive, and the realization of what it meant to look into the eyes of the dead boy's mother and father started to sink in.

"On the day of the meeting, the inmate could only cry. He kept cowering, unable to look into their eyes. The parents sat there for about ten minutes just looking at him. Suddenly, the wife walked toward him and yelled, 'GET UP!' I was unsure of what was going to happen next. The inmate stood up, prepared for an assault. The wife simply opened her arms and hugged him. After a few minutes, the husband followed suit. It was one of the most touching moments I'd ever witnessed. Not long after, the parents began to write the inmate and send him scripture passages. Soon they made weekly trips to the prison to visit him. I remember asking the wife how they were able to suppress their loss. Wasn't seeing the inmate a painful reminder? The wife told me that seeing goodness in a man she thought was evil lets her know that there is a God, and moreover, that their son is with Him. After months of letters and visits, the inmate now trusted them. He asked the boy's parents if they could reach out to his estranged son, after fearing he was on the same path. They honored his request and have since built a relationship with his son. Though his son will never make up for their loss, it has helped the healing process. It all began with forgiveness."

Her mom reached for Sarah's hands and held them tight. Sarah could feel her mom trembling.

"I'm sorry. I'm so, so sorry for what I have put you through." Her voice quivered and tears ran down her face as she spoke. "I wished it were me that died. I drank myself half to death and tried hard to make that happen. I didn't deserve to live, Sarah… But I did. So, I vowed to be a better person. Change my life. My life could no longer be my own–it had to be His. That was the only way to make anything right."

Sarah listened to her mother and knew she had to forgive her. She was tired of resenting her. It had been too long. It hurt too much to keep holding on to the grief when God was telling her to let it go. Sarah wrapped her arms around her mom, squeezed tight, and wept.

"I love you, mom. I… forgive you."

Her mother held her child for a long time. She needed to make up for a decade of lost embraces.

***

Sarah had been relaxed for the few days she was at her mother's home. Her mother's house-phone rang, Sarah answered it.

"Hello… Hello…" There was only silence on the other end.

Andrew placed the receiver down and slowly looked forward at Jade.

"Yes, she's at her mother's house. Are you going to tell me what you want with her, now?" Andrew asked Jade out of genuine concern.

"I was given a directive from Samuel Linden to find her. She has been working on a deal with DeAmato, and we have not been able to contact her." Jade said casually.

Andrew did not like Jade. He remembered him getting close to Sarah at the Gala and had a strong feeling they had been romantically involved. However, he was a brother, and the brotherhood stood before all else. That was part of the sworn oath Andrew willingly took.

The wheels in Jade's head began spinning.

"You could be of even greater assistance... Interested in moving up in the Order?" Jade asked as he casually glanced at his ring.

Andrew was more than interested. Andrew imagined himself wearing the GMA ring and being worshipped, idolized, and envied just as he had done for years; longing for an opportunity such as this to present itself. Andrew could feel the cold gold wrapped around his finger.

That night Sarah turned on her cell phone and listened to her voicemail. The mailbox was full. There were several messages from Detective Staller.

"Sarah, please give us a call. You need to be in protective custody. DeAmato is a dangerous man with many connections and he's on the loose."

Sarah was happy at her mother's home and wanted—and needed—to stay. Sarah, determined not to live in fear, deleted the messages.

*"You are of your father the devil, and your will is to do your father's desires. He was a murderer from the beginning, and has nothing to do with the truth, because there is no truth in him. When he lies, he speaks out of his own character, for he is a liar and the father of lies." John 8:44*

# Chapter Nineteen

## The Cost

It had only been a month since the presentation, and Sarah valued every moment spent with her mother. Trips to the grocery store, Bible study, and hour-long conversations suddenly meant so much. The two of them prayed together for hours. Most times they just praised Him. But there were times Sarah just needed to be by herself in the presence of God.

Her first real prayer by herself was the most honest she had ever been. She asked for forgiveness for all her sins—adultery, anger, envy, lust, and vanity. She cried for a long time that night as prayer became a cathartic release of pent up tension and stress. Each day as she prayed, she started to just listen and use her senses to take in signs from God. She sat in silence on her mom's veranda and studied scripture. She'd read a chapter or two and took a moment to think about the lessons. Her life was never this calm.

She was always striving for the next goal or the next challenge. She never took the time to appreciate what she had. As she read more of God's word and listened more, she began to feel she had enough. She found the meaning of contentment.

The happiness Sarah felt could not overpower the eerie feeling that kept eating away at her. As each day passed, she felt like her time was coming to an end. But she wasn't afraid.

As she helped her mom with dinner there was a friendly knock on the door. Sarah opened it.

"Andrew..." She whispered. Sarah was shocked, but realized he was the only person who knew her mom's location.

"Yes, Sarah. It seems as though I must always make bold moves just to see you."

Sarah blushed. Andrew was still very charming.

"What are you doing in New Haven?" Sarah asked.

"Well, I am in town for a seminar; I thought I would just see if you were here. I guess the long shot paid off."

She smiled at Andrew as she fought back the old feelings for him that invaded her thoughts.

"So... Would you like to get a drink with me? I promise I'll have you back before twelve." Andrew said jokingly.

Sarah laughed and grabbed her coat.

***

They were seated at a booth and spoke to each other like nothing happened. In that moment, nothing seemed to matter and there was no animosity. Andrew did not bring up Sarah's disappearance after the Gala, and they spoke openly about a number of issues never addressed in their relationship.

"Andrew... I've changed." Sarah said candidly.

"How have you changed?" Andrew asked.

Sarah shrugged her shoulders.

"I don't know. The things I valued for so long are not important to me anymore. I don't think David Mercer is a jerk either."

Andrew almost choked on his wine.

"Really?" Andrew said, "Now *that* is truly commendable."

They both began laughing and Andrew stopped abruptly as though a thought interrupted his apparent happiness.

"What's wrong?" Sarah asked.

"Nothing… I am just very glad to see you, Sarah." Andrew said as he caressed her hands. Sarah pulled away.

"This isn't right, Andrew…"

Andrew nodded with an understanding of what she meant.

"I have to start all over. I wasted so much time reverting back to unhealthy behavior and hoping for a different result. I need to find the loving, kindhearted, God-centered woman I used to be. That's the only thing that is important to me now. Hopefully, I have enough time." Sarah said half-jokingly.

Sarah leaned over and gave Andrew one final kiss on the cheek. He looked at her, and his eyes watered a bit.

***

When they sat in the car, the two exchanged a look of affection. A song came on that Sarah liked, and she sang along. Andrew turned it off. Sarah looked at Andrew who was focused on the road. "Everything OK?" Andrew didn't respond. Sarah felt that eerie feeling again. She noticed a car following closely. The person driving turned on the high beams blinding Andrew.

"What in the hell is this guy's problem!?" Andrew yelled.

Without warning, the car rammed the back of Andrew's car. Sarah screamed and turned back. The car approached on the passenger's side and began shoving Andrew's car violently. In an effort to avoid oncoming traffic, Andrew swerved off the road into a ditch. He put the car in reverse and immediately began pressing the gas, but nothing was happening. In the rearview mirror, Sarah could see a group of men, dressed entirely in black, approaching the car.

"Andrew, we have to run!" Sarah said as she tried to push the jammed door open. When she finally managed to break through, with just enough time to run, it was of no use. A large man wrapped his arms around her chest restricting her movement. Sarah screamed and kicked as hard as she could. The man placed a cloth with a strange substance over her nose and mouth. Her field of vision darkened, and she lost consciousness.

***

Sarah was awakened by cold water thrown in her face. She was seated on a chair with her arms and feet tied tightly to it. Sarah began to struggle; however, the more she moved, the more pain she felt as the rope cut into her ankles and wrists.

"HELP ME!!" She screamed until her voice cracked.

All she could hear was laughter and mumbling in the room. She could barely see anyone. The room was so dark that she could only make out the outlines of bodies. She saw a light far down a hallway that seemed to grow brighter as it got closer. For a moment she thought she might have been dead. A man with a long, black cloak entered the room with a torch. The man let his torch, touch another torch and the fire was passed down the line. Sarah could now see everyone. There were twelve men dressed in black cloaks forming a circle around her. Sarah was terrified.

"WHERE AM I? WHAT'S GOING ON?" Sarah screamed.

There was no answer. The men remained with their heads down. The first man approached her, then removed his hood. Sarah gasped. It was Jade.

"WHAT ARE YOU DOING? LET ME GO!"

Jade gently put one finger over his mouth.

"Shhh…"

Jade lifted his hand and smacked her across the face. The act dazed her into silence.

Jade began to speak.

"We are gathered here today because our brother has the opportunity to reach the highest level of enlightenment in the order. We all know this awareness comes with a price. In order to truly understand the complexities of this world and the universe and reap its benefits, one must willingly give up their humanity in order to become a god. To be a god, you must feel the power of life in your hands and have the courage to take that life. That is the sacrifice."

Upon hearing this, Sarah began screaming uncontrollably. One of the cloaked men tied a cloth around her mouth to muffle the screams. One final man entered the room. It was Andrew. Sarah began to sob, now aware of his betrayal. Jade whispered something in his ear and then stepped back as though he was about to watch a show.

"Now, we will commence with the power of twelve. Each cloaked man will hit her exactly twelve times. We will go around this circle repeating the process until she is dead." Jade said.

Sarah tried to break free but to no avail. The first punch to her stomach was the worst pain she had ever felt. The beating continued for hours. Some men took their time and would break between blows. There were moments when she fell out of consciousness, and an extreme blow to the head woke her back up. She wished it would all end. As though someone read her thoughts, suddenly, it all stopped. Sarah was untied around the sixth round of the beating and her limp body fell to the ground. She was presented with an option.

"At this point, you can put yourself out of your own misery or continue feeling the worst pain I am certain you have ever felt." Jade said.

Jade had a gun with a single bullet. It hurt for Sarah to breathe. Her ribs and nose felt broken. All she could taste was her own blood and her eyes were swollen. Her eyelids opened just enough to see the pain she was enduring. Jade handed her the gun and helped her grab it. She considered the offer. The pain she felt was more than she could bear; she wanted to die. Her eyes closed, and she mumbled something. Jade could not hear. He placed his face close to her mouth.

"What's that, Sarah?"

She continued murmuring. Jade put his ear close enough to hear. She was saying, "God, save me." In that instant, she released her hand from the gun. Jade knew that she was not going to kill herself. He picked up the gun and handed it to Andrew.

"Kill her, or we will beat her to death."

Andrew looked at Sarah, who was unrecognizable now. Andrew's hand shook as he pointed the gun at her head. Sarah did not cry. She did not beg for her life. She just stared deep into his eyes. A strange calmness entered her body, and she no longer felt any pain. She thought about her husband and the possibility of seeing him again.

Andrew knew the image of her looking at him would never leave his mind. He pulled the trigger and released a single shot, killing her. Samuel Linden removed his hood and pulled a black case out of his pocket. It was a GMA ring. He approached Andrew and placed the ring on his finger. Samuel's hand was still covered with Sarah's blood. Samuel shook Andrew's hand in a symbolic gesture, transferring the blood to Andrew's hands. Eleven other men followed suit. Andrew was given a cloak and was handed a lit torch. He now understood the significance. Each man in that room went through the same initiation. He could never know what powers and secrets the world had to offer unless he was prepared to take a life and have a secret of his own. Samuel Linden patted Andrew on the back.

"Do not worry; your secrets are safe with us. Now the world is yours." He said.

Jade stood next to Sarah and gazed at her lifeless corpse. He was disappointed that he was unable to encourage her suicide. Satan appeared in his human form; Jade was terrified.

"I'm coming back, aren't I?" Jade asked.

"No, I will keep you here for a bit. I have plans for you."

"Did I get her soul?" Jade asked.

"I am not sure yet," Satan replied. "God must judge her first."

***

Meanwhile, packages with disks arrived on the desk of the Editor and Chief of the Post, an Italian Policeman, and Officer Staller of the DCPD.

*If you are reading this, I'm probably dead. I'm a person who, for a number of years, has only used my conscience when it suited me best. I can no longer do this. I'm not sure what any of this will do, but I am praying that it will do something. You have the information, now it is up to you to spread the word. Military weaponry like the Annihilator is being created every day. It is becoming more advanced, and the human cost is more than we can afford. Not just for those who are killed, also for the operators. The operators who pull the triggers, press the buttons, and create catastrophic loss of life lose their humanity as well. I pray that this video footage from Future Intellect Inc. starts a chain of events that sheds light on the military technology we purchase and sell and the ethical considerations therein.*

*-Sarah Michel*

Satan rested his arm on Jade's shoulder. Jade possibly lost a soul—the first one since he'd been on earth. That bothered him. Satan told Jade to close his eyes.

"Imagine your enemies sleeping peacefully on a battlefield. Do you see how vulnerable they are? Imagine all the things you could do to them. You could end their lives before they even wake up. That's power. That's control. You have the advantage. Humanity is in a deep slumber. Their eyes are closed while war is waged for their souls. They are blissfully unaware—most unconcerned with what's at stake."

Satan took a seat. Jade opened his eyes and sat down as well.

"Their souls are more valuable than gold, more precious than water, and amazingly, they are willing to leave it unprotected for the taking." Satan laughed.

"Look at how far we've come. We've gotten them to worship anything and everything else, but God. What do you want to worship today? Idols? How about more than one god? Things? Stuff? Money? Yourself? Sure! Whatever you like!"

They gazed at the stars in the sky. It was a beautiful night. The two were quiet for a moment and took it all in.

"You know God's chosen people don't even know who they are?" Satan added. "They were enslaved, tortured, hung, and imprisoned, and now they are killed daily and no one cares. We dehumanize and humiliate them every chance we get and so does everyone else. We've convinced them they are so worthless they hate everything about themselves. Do you see the irony in that? God's chosen people—the first people—the people from whom the rest of humanity spawned... hate themselves."

Jade leaned back and really thought about what Satan was saying for the first time. He had never seen God or his Son, but Satan certainly had. It seemed to reason that the people who would endure the most abuse would have the closest resemblance to God.

"We are legislating sin—you can legally kill, and steal. We've managed to create various exceptions for breaking two commandments."

Jade was impressed. He lived in an era where these things were done in secret. There were back-room deals. Under-the-table exchanges, but this was never openly accepted.

"How'd you manage that?" Jade asked.

"Well, we've figured out that you just have to rename it and attach a liberty interest. Voila! What was once wrong now becomes debatable."

Jade was processing all of this. Much of what Satan was saying didn't make sense. Everything seemed so backwards and turned around. Jade certainly wasn't complaining. This was going to guarantee his stay on earth.

"If it wasn't already abundantly clear, don't fret over the loss of one or even a few. There will be some that wake up, but there are billions, sleeping peacefully. We're winning." Satan said.

"What is your plan for me?" Jade asked.

"I've done some of my best work here in America. I want you to stay here. You were a Statesman before; let's make you a Statesman again. But first… Some required reading…"

Satan pressed the cover of a leather-bound book against Jade's chest. When he turned the book down the cover read, "Holy Bible."

Jade looked at Satan perplexed. Satan laughed at his reaction.

"Hey… even liars know the truth."

Just like that, Satan disappeared.

***

Jade could see dawn breaking through the clouds. It was a new day, and he was ready to conquer the world.

The End

# __Acknowledgments__

Dear God, Yahweh, all the glory belongs to You. I could have achieved nothing in my life without first knowing You. Thank You for your grace, your forgiveness, and your protection.

My parents were God's first blessing to me. They taught me love, kindness, and respect. My first glimpse of God was through them. They gave me the foundation to become the person God wanted.

My brother always protected me. His presence in my life strengthened me. He is the greatest gift a sister could have.

My family gave me confidence. The legacy started by my grandparents, my aunts, uncles, and cousins instilled in me a strong sense of pride in who I am. They cared for me, prayed for me, fed me, and supported me. I was blessed to be a part of a family so special.

My friends have been there when I needed them and even when I didn't know I needed them. I thank them for the laughs, the inside jokes, the discussions, the gatherings, and much needed support.

Join the Aknowingspirit community!

Facebook: Aknowingspirit
FB Discussion group: Aknowingspirit speaks!
Twitter: @Aknowingspirit
Instagram: @Aknowingspirit
Subscribe to the newsletter! Visit **www.aknowingspirit.com**

Look forward to connecting with you!

aknowingspirit

www.ingramcontent.com/pod-product-compliance
Lightning Source LLC
Chambersburg PA
CBHW021200110726
47900CB00002B/664